The Watch

Robert Westall was born in 1929 on Tyneside, where he grew up during the Second World War. He studied Fine Art at Durham University, and Sculpture at the Slade in London, before teaching art in schools in the North of England. He was also a branch director of the Samaritans, a journalist and an antique dealer. Between 1985 and his death in 1993, he retired to devote himself to his writing.

His first novel for children, *The Machine Gunners*, published by Macmillan in 1975, won the Carnegie Medal. He won it again in 1982 for *The Scarecrows* (the first writer to win the medal twice), the Smarties Prize in 1989 for *Blitzcat*, and the Guardian Award in 1991 for *The Kingdom by the Sea*.

Reviews of Robert Westall's work:

'A writer who managed to combine literary excellence with an immense talent for capturing the imagination and interest of child and, in particular, young adult readers.'
Independent

'Westall was a writer of rare talent. We shall miss him, but he has left us such a wonderful legacy.'
Michael Morpurgo, *Guardian*

Books by Robert Westall

Fiction

Blitz
Blitzcat
Blizzard
Break of Dark
The Call and Other Stories
The Cats of Seroster
The Creature in the Dark
The Christmas Cat
The Christmas Ghost
Christmas Spirit
The Creature in the Dark
Demons and Shadows
The Devil on the Road
Echoes of War
Falling into Glory
Fathom Five
Fearful Lovers
Futuretrack Five
Ghost Abbey
Ghosts and Journeys
Gulf
Harvest
The Haunting of Chas McGill
If Cats Could Fly
The Kingdom by the Sea
Love Match
The Machine Gunners
The Night Mare
Old Man on a Horse
A Place for Me
The Promise

Rachel and the Angel
The Scarecrows
Size Twelve
The Stones of Muncaster
  Cathedral
Stormsearch
A Time of Fire
Urn Burial
Voices in the Wind
A Walk on the Wild Side
The Watch House
The Wheatstone Pond
The Wind Eye
The Witness
Yaxley's Cat

For adults

Antique Dust

Anthologies

Cats' Whispers and Tales
Ghost Stories
The Best of Robert Westall
  Volume One: Demons and
  Shadows
The Best of Robert Westall
  Volume Two: Shades of
  Darkness

Non-fiction

Children of the Blitz

The Watch House

Robert Westall

MACMILLAN CHILDREN'S BOOKS

First published 1977 by Macmillan London Ltd

This edition published 2002 by Macmillan Children's Books
a division of Macmillan Publishers Limited
20 New Wharf Road, London N1 9RR
Basingstoke and Oxford
www.panmacmillan.com

Associated companies throughout the world

ISBN 0 330 39863 6

1 3 5 7 9 8 6 4 2

A CIP catalogue record for this book is available from
the British Library

Typeset by Intype London Ltd
Printed and bound in Great Britain by Mackays of Chatham plc, Kent

For Chris, my son, and my companion in the Watch House

PART ONE

Over what bones is built my house,
Who waits for Judgement Day to come,
Who rests, but does not rest in peace
And fills with whispers all this room?

From whose heart springs the bending rose
That spills red petals on the green?
Who stands behind the window pane –
A face familiar but unseen?

C. Makepeace

1

They were driving into Garmouth before Mother said defensively:

'You do remember Prudie, don't you?'

''Course I remember Prudie,' snapped Anne. 'She did look after me till I was eight.'

'I've seen her since,' said Mother. 'She's changed. Her hair's gone grey.' Mother made it sound like the end of the world; for Mother it would have been.

'But I'm sure she'll look after you,' added Mother, 'like she always did.'

'Yes,' said Anne, flatly.

'I'm grateful to Prudie for taking you, of course. But I'll not pretend she's ideal. She knows her place. But Arthur, that brother of hers . . . A waster. Never made anything of himself, even by *their* standards. He takes advantage, given half a chance. You'll need to watch him.'

'What is he – a rapist?'

'I wish you wouldn't talk like that.'

The sea came into view, at the end of Front Street, Garmouth.

'I had such *fun* here, as a child,' said Mother, 'just after the War. Prudie took me to the beach every sunny day, when she was *my* nanny. This was all seaside-shops then. Buckets and spades, and those windmill-things you hold in your hand.'

3

Anne eyed three pubs, a Roman Catholic church and presbytery, and the front of the Carlton Cinema. All obviously pre-war. Mother was having her fantasy of innocent childhood again.

They turned right at the Victoria Jubilee Clock Tower, and plunged down steeply. Anne gasped with pleasure. They were running down into a deep little bay between the two great headlands.

The headland on the left was red sandstone, with red sandstone ruins on top. Ruins like crumbling hands, with fingers pointing skywards. Ruins with pointed gables and empty lancet windows. Just enough left to imagine the ghost of a great church.

Below the ruins, on the incredibly green grass, huddled an army of tombstones: some red like the ruins, some black obelisks, and the occasional glitter of white marble. They clustered right to the edge of the cliff. The sea must eat away the cliff, thought Anne. Some wild nights, bones long buried in earth must receive final burial in the sea.

'Garmouth Priory,' said Mother. 'Where all the old sea-captains are buried.'

At the bottom of the hill, they rumbled across a wooden bridge. Looking over the side, Anne saw a disused railway-track, smothered in brambles.

'That's the old wagon-way,' said Mother. 'You'll have lots to explore.'

The car began to climb up on to the further headland. This was emptier; just one long white building on top.

'That's them,' said Mother.

'Prudie? In that big house?'

Mother laughed unkindly. 'Oh, they don't *live*

4

there. That's Brigade Watch House. They live behind, in Brigade Cottage.'

The road ended at the Watch House, which loomed over them as they got out of the car. Built of long white planks, sagging with the years, it had a maritime look. Like a mastless roofed-in schooner becalmed in a sea of dead grass. Single-storey like a church hall. Through its windows showed a dark clutter of things that couldn't be recognized. This clutter and a lack of curtains made the windows look like eyes in a white planked face.

On the right, a wing stuck out. Anne could make out a rack of billiard-cues inside, and a billiard-table under a green cover.

At the far end was a white planked tower, also full of windows. Anne felt a delicious little shudder. The Watch House was well-named. It did seem to watch you. But it was only the effect of dark windows in white walls.

The dead grass of the garden revealed hints of wreckage. Flaked white railings struggled up, only to collapse groundwards in long loops. There were rusty things among the grass-roots; anchors, chains, something that might be a cannon.

At the end of the garden, the cliff-edge dropped sheer to the blue distances of the River Gar, with tugboats moving, smaller than toys.

There was an entrance in the base of the tower. Just beyond, a great wooden figure thrust upwards through the grass. A ship's figurehead; a warrior with cracked shield and broken helmet. The body was weathered grey by wind and rain, but it was the bearded face that intrigued Anne. It was lined and

5

seamed like an old man's face and the eyes were dark and living. She waded towards it through the long grass.

Close to, she saw the expression on the face was an illusion; the wood had cracked, and rotted inside the cracks. Eyes and mouth were pits of damp decay, in which woodlice crawled.

She reached up and touched the face, and a piece of wood came away in her hand, and crumbled to brown dirt between her fingers.

The whole thing was ready to fall apart. And yet it loomed over her with all the thrusting power of the great ship it had once belonged to.

She wiped the brown stain off her fingers on to her jeans, with a grimace of disgust.

'Stop dreaming,' called Mother crossly, from the other end of the garden. 'I haven't got all day.' The vista of the Gar made her look creased and artificial, like a hothouse daffodil.

They walked round the Watch House, Anne humping her suitcase. They passed a sign saying *To Brigade Cottage* in straggly letters. Then there was a low roof behind a trellis and another straggly notice saying *Ring for Attention*.

Mother pushed open the trellis-gate. It gave on to a backyard, in which a man was shaving, mirror propped on a windowsill. The mirror carried the legend *Player's Navy Cut* and a sailor's head inside a lifebelt. The man crouched in his vest, peering through the gaps in the lifebelt with great concentration. His braces hung in loops over his trousers. As he wielded his razor, dollops of foam fell into an enamel basin, to the deep fascination of a ginger cat that sat watching.

'Hang on, hinny. With you in a sec,' called the man, without turning. He had white hair and a wrinkled neck. But his movements were deft and young.

Then the back door flew open, jogging his elbow. Blood ran down his cheek, staining the foam pink.

'Bugger,' said the man without heat. 'Aah wish ye wouldn't do that, Prudie. Third time this week.'

'And Aah wish ye'd get shaved in the bathroom like a Christian.'

'Too dark in the bathroom.'

'Not if ye used the proper mirror.'

'George Jobling gave me this mirror, year o' the General Strike. Out of his Da's shop.'

'That's—' Prudie's head emerged round the door, with a pair of wet socks. 'Why, it's Miss Fiona and the bairn! Couldn't you see who it was, Arthur? What you want to keep Miss Fiona waiting in the yard for? Men . . .' She put the wet socks on the windowsill, and patted her hair with a sudsy hand. 'Come in if you can get!'

They pushed through a passage hung with enough oilskins and reefer-jackets to equip the Navy.

'Ye mustn't mind Arthur,' said Prudie. 'He can never bring hisself to throw anything away. That's his Granda's sou'wester there.'

The living room of Brigade Cottage was small as a ship's cabin. An oil-lamp hung from the ceiling. There was a roaring fire in spite of the heat of the day, set around with brass ornaments that shone like silver. And on the oil-cloth of the table, plates of scones and tarts and egg-custards giving off a symphony of glorious smells.

'You'll stay . . . ?' asked Prudie.

'Just a cup of tea for me,' said Mother. 'I must watch my figure now I'm a working girl again.' She slipped a thin tube of saccharine from her handbag.

Prudie turned abruptly to the kettle on the hob; but it didn't hide the disappointed droop in her shoulders.

'I'm famished,' said Anne. 'I could eat a horse. Can I start?'

'*Anne*,' said Mother in horror. 'Wait till you're asked. And don't start filling yourself up with starch. You're overweight already and it'll only start your spots again.'

'Aaah, she's a growing bairn,' said Prudie, smiling again.

Arthur came in. He must have finished shaving like greased lightning. He'd stuck a piece of newspaper over the cut on his chin, to stop the bleeding. He sat down in the corner, blue eyes fixed on Mother with the intentness of a dog expecting a bone. Mother quivered visibly in protest.

'Arthur . . .' said Prudie beseechingly.

'Give us a spot o' tea, wumman.' He lifted a pint-pot off a hook and plonked it down among the more delicate china. Then he took a pipe out of his pocket and began rubbing dark tobacco between his hands.

'Arthur,' wailed Prudie again.

'What?' asked Arthur innocently. This was a game that had been played out many times before.

'Don't mind *me*,' said Mother. 'I need a cigarette too . . . oh!' She displayed an empty gold cigarette-case with a helpless gesture. 'I meant to get some!'

'Arthur, run up Front Street and get Miss Fiona some cigarettes.'

'Hold on. Aah haven't had me tea yet.'

'It's gone five. Shops'll be shut in a minute.'

'Aah'll go to the pub.'

'You get in that pub an' you won't come back.'

'Oh, don't bother,' said Mother in her best Christian-martyr voice. 'I'll try and get some on the motorway.'

'You've got forty in the glove compartment. Don't you remember?' said Anne. You cow, she thought.

'Oh, *those*,' said Mother. 'I can't smoke *those*. My throat's sore. I need some Menthol.'

But Arthur's departure didn't satisfy her. 'That's enough food, Anne. You'll make yourself sick. Go and unpack.'

'But I'm not *finished*!'

'Bring the jam tarts along with you, hinny,' said Prudie. 'Aah'll have to throw them in the bin, else.' She picked up Anne's case and led her through a small gleaming mahogany door on the right of the fireplace.

But the plate of tarts didn't placate Anne. Nor the spotless bedroom with a porthole for a window. Nor the bed like a ship's bunk, with brass-handled drawers beneath.

Mother had got her own way, as she always did. Mother was playing at being a little girl with her nanny again; being comforted that everything was all right when everything was far from all right. And Mother would be slandering Daddy.

Anne flung herself on the patchwork quilt and put her ear to the white boards of the wall. In time to hear Mother say, '. . . totally impossible. He's gone

9

too far this time. *He* has to try and market a new carburettor, right in the middle of a recession. Then he has cash-flow problems, like I told him he would. So d'you know what he's *done*? Mortgaged the house for forty thousand pounds, to pour into that *bloody* factory.'

Prudie's voice was softer, soothing. Good old Nanny. Anne couldn't make out the words. Then Mother's sharpness again.

'What is there to be patient *for*? I never see him. He never takes me anywhere. Never home till midnight, then it's a couple of drinks and snoring in an armchair. I'm still a young woman . . .'

Murmur, murmur. The soft answer that turneth away wrath.

'No. I've told him it's final. That house was the only reason I stayed. That and the garden. I worked so hard on that garden. And he had no right . . . my solicitor says half of it belonged to *me*.'

Anne buried her face in the pillow. Fastened her teeth into it as if she could tear it in half. Oh, Daddy, Daddy. Daddy lying asleep on the couch downstairs in the early mornings. Making him coffee. Trying to talk to him, cheer him up, while he stared blankly at the wall. Daddy asking painful forced questions about ponies and school, and not even listening to the answers. Daddy even trying to be polite to horrible sly Uncle Monty. Daddy, will you *never* stand up for yourself?

Then the shouting-match last night. Nosy as Anne was, she had stopped listening after an hour. She had pulled the blankets over her head to block out the noise.

10

Then early this morning: Daddy gone and Mother standing by her bed in a house-coat. Get up, Anne. Get dressed, Anne. We're leaving, Anne.

No point in arguing. Mother had left before. That time, there was a court proceeding, and Mother got something called Care and Custody. Which meant Anne had to do what Mother said. Daddy hadn't even appeared in court to dispute it.

No time even to say goodbye to Toby, grazing in the orchard. Toby glimpsed through the car window, lifting his head from the dew-laden grass, looking hopeful . . .

And here she was, dumped on Prudie for a whole summer. Like a *parcel*.

Anne jammed her head against the wall again. Mother was saying, in more reasonable tones, 'Can I give you something for her keep? I'm a little pushed for money at the moment but . . .'

Prudie making certainly-not noises. A pleasure to have the bairn . . . like old times.

Prudie and Arthur on their pensions and Mother with a purse stuffed with tenners. Anne smashed her fists into the pillow again.

Tapping on the door.

'Miss Anne . . . your mother's going.'

Anne pulled her face from the warm damp pillow with a start. At first she couldn't remember where she was. Then she realized the room was darker, and looked at her watch. Half past eight.

She'd slept, while Daddy was being slandered. Even though she'd been awake since six that morning, she still felt guilty.

She dipped her hand in the ewer of water and sloshed the tears off her face. She scrubbed away with a towel, but her face still looked terrible. Prudie knew, as soon as Anne opened the door. You could never hide anything from Prudie. Prudie's warm sadness descended on Anne like a blanket. Added to her own, it was nearly unbearable.

'You'll be all right then?' asked Mother, rattling her car-keys and already halfway to London in her mind.

Anne just looked at her. Prudie made little helpless motions, like smoothing a pillow.

Arthur appeared with the Menthol cigarettes, outrageously late, unrepentant, and with the smell of whisky on his breath.

'How much do I owe you?' asked Mother coldly.

'Be my guest,' said Arthur, in a tone that made Mother look at him sharply.

'You'll be in touch then, Miss Fiona?' asked Prudie.

They all went out and watched, while Mother backed and turned the yellow Sunbeam Alpine. Then she was off, never looking back.

Which was perhaps as well. Arthur wrinkled his nose at Mother's back. Then muttered, quite distinctly:

'Good riddance to bad rubbish.'

Prudie gave him a look. Arthur rolled his eyes in schoolboy guilt.

Anne burst out laughing. Prudie gave her a worried glance, as if she might be sickening for something.

'Come'n have some supper, pet,' she said soothingly.

12

'I want to show her the Watch House,' protested Arthur.

'What's she want to see your old rubbish for?'

'S'not old rubbish. S'educational,' roared Arthur.

'It's all right for you and your old cronies. It's not fit for a young girl.'

Arthur fixed Anne with his expectant doggy look.

'Please, Prudie, I *would* like to see the Watch House,' said Anne, with maximum politeness.

'Oh, suit yourself,' said Prudie. But she wasn't pleased.

2

Arthur pressed a light-switch. Dim electric lights came on down the long high hall. Two of them flickered off again.

'Wiring's bad,' said Arthur. 'It all needs re-doing, but we haven't got the money.' He banged the wall by the light-switch. The two delinquent lights flickered briefly. 'I'll have to have another go at them,' said Arthur. 'But I'm not much cop at wiring.'

The missing lights were needed. Light was already fading over the wide mouth of the Gar. The long room would soon be dark, in spite of its many windows.

The roof was high and shadowed. From its rafters hung many strange objects looking down like angels in a church. There was a broken ship's wheel; half a rim and three battered spokes. There were the name-plates of ships. *HMS Iron Crown* and the *First of May* and the *Cactus* of Blyth. The name-plate of the *City of Bristol* was held up by two naked nymphs, fat, ill-carved and repainted shocking pink. There were two huge rusty tin-cans.

Arthur saw her looking at the tin-cans. 'Them saved a man's life,' he said. 'He was the captain of the *Jurneeks* of Riga. He held one under each arm and jumped into the waves and drifted to shore.'

Anne advanced down the room. From the walls, figureheads stared. They weren't brightly-coloured

14

like the ones at Greenwich. These had been white-washed, for convenience sake. It gave them a grave-yard look, glimmering in the gloom.

Sightless white eyes stared.

The ones at Greenwich had been restored; had all their arms and legs. But these were still maimed by the violence of the sea.

A headless mermaid.

A general, split from throat to crutch and half his body gone.

A buxom lady with pouting lips and a rose between her breasts. Snapped off at the waist. And the hand that held the rose had no arm.

Under the whitewash, there was agony in the splinters.

They're only wood, thought Anne. But she went on tiptoe.

All down the left-hand side of the room were tables carrying models, mainly old ships in glass cases. Down the right, a long clutter of ropes, pulleys and metal boxes.

'*The gear of foreign dead men,*' said Anne to herself.

'Yewhat?' asked Arthur.

'Just a poem I once read,' said Anne. 'By T. S. Eliot.'

'I knew a feller called Tommy Elliot,' said Arthur. 'He was drowned behind the North Pier in 1932.'

'What *is* this place?' asked Anne. 'What *is* the Watch House?'

Arthur squared his shoulders and put on an official voice. 'The Watch House is the property of Garmouth Volunteer Life Brigade.' This was obviously a speech

15

he'd made many times before. 'The Life Brigade was founded in 1870, for the saving of shipwrecked mariners.'

'Shipwrecked where?' asked Anne, staring out of the window at the little bay with its broad sandy beach and a man throwing sticks for his frantic dog.

'Not there, hinny,' said Arthur. 'That bay's safe as houses. Bairns of five can bathe there in all weathers. But look at this.' He led her back to the tower end of the Watch House, that overlooked the river. He pointed past the figurehead of the warrior in the garden.

Below the cliff, the evening blueness of the Gar was marred by two immense stretches of dirty black rock. Each had a post at its furthest tip, bearing a metal basket.

'*These* rocks?' asked Anne, wonderingly. 'They don't look dangerous. They look like someone's been tipping rubbish in the river!'

'Aye,' said Arthur grimly. 'That's mebbe why the near ones is called the Black Middens. A midden was where you put rubbish before folks had dustbins. The rocks further out to sea is called the Battery Rocks, 'cos a battery of guns was put there, against the Spanish Armada.'

'But they all look so flat and smooth!'

'Aye, till twenty-foot waves picks up a ship and drops it on top of them. Then it picks it up an' drops it again. Like smashing a coconut on a doorstep. One south-east gale, we lost twenty-seven fishing-smacks in one day. Aall the men drooned, within sight of their own front door. Aall the wives watchin' from

16

this cliff, and the cliff too steep an' high for anyone to help.'

'How could a Life Brigade help, then?'

Arthur marched her down the hall again, nearly to the door marked *Billiard Room*.

'By using a breeches-buoy. Aah've made a model of it, here. To show visitors, like.'

The model was ten feet long. Mostly plaster sea with incredibly high and neatly-painted waves. On the right, a shattered sailing-ship lay on the rocks. On the left was a plaster cliff. From a tripod on the cliff, three ropes went to the doomed vessel. Hanging from the ropes, in a little canvas sling, sat an Action Man wearing a ridiculous hand-knitted sailor's cap.

Arthur turned a little handle on the tripod. Action Man began to travel jerkily from ship to shore, heels tapping against the tops of the plaster waves. He reached the cliff and Arthur turned the handle the other way, returning him to his place of peril.

'Ye fire a rocket out to the ship, wi' a rope attached called a whip. The ship's crew haul on the whip to fetch across the breeches-buoy. Here, try it.'

Anne dutifully turned the handle. Action Man returned, with a tiny hollow knocking.

'Not to scale, o' course,' said Arthur modestly. 'That's a real breeches-buoy there.' He pointed to an array of ropes, pulleys and metal boxes. And to a blackboard carrying that same straggly lettering.

Monthly rocket-drill, 4th of August.

'You still practise, then?' asked Anne.

'Aye,' said Arthur bitterly. 'Not that there's much point these days. When they built the piers, they pulled the Midden's teeth. D'you see?' He pointed a calloused finger.

The whole mouth of the Gar, and the little bay below, were enclosed between long grey granite piers. One thrust out from Priory Cliff. Another from the south bank of the river.

'Our pier's half-a-mile long, an' the South Shields one, three-quarters. They break the force of the waves. An' again, steamers don't get in trouble like sailing-ships used to. An' what wi' radar . . .'

'You don't see much action?'

'Oh, ships still run aground, even wi' radar. Specially in fog. But the waves don't smash them up any more. Usually they're floated off wi' the next tide. We still turn out the lads an' get the breeches-buoy across, but ship's crews don't seem to fancy using it any more – specially after dark. Usually they wait till low-tide an' walk ashore. They come to thank us after, like. But our lads get discouraged, what wi' helicopters an' all that sort of Modern Thinking.' Arthur nearly spat on the floor, till he remembered himself. 'They should turn this place into a museum. That's all its fit for now. Aah build a few models to attract visitors. Lookit this here – St Mary's lighthouse.'

And there was a plaster island, emerald-green, complete with white tower and blue-painted toy soldiers peering out to sea.

'The light flashes and turns, all correct,' said Arthur, pressing a switch. The light turned and flashed once, then stopped.

'That needs seeing to an' all,' said Arthur.

'D'you get many visitors?'

18

'We had two, last Easter Monday.'

'Oh!'

'We been passed by. Lack of money and Modern Thinking. Aah keep writing to headmasters, asking them to send classes down. But they don't seem over-interested. It's a long walk for the bairns. And they've no idea how much is here. . .'

Arthur pointed to a brass porthole, with a water-colour of a ship inset. 'That's the *Stanley* – iron-screw steamer. Went aground on the Black Middens, November 1864, about dusk. Thirty passengers, twenty-seven crew, forty-seven head of cattle. That was the worst night. South Shields lifeboat couldn't put to sea for the waves, an' the Garmouth lifeboat lost all her oars an' two good lads. Twenty-four drooned in the *Stanley* an' six in the schooner *Friendship* ashore on the Battery Rocks at the same time.'

'But why do all these relics end up *here*?'

Arthur pushed back his sailor's cap and scratched his head.

'Aah never gave that much thought. Aah suppose the Brigade lads in the early days . . . picked up souvenirs, like. Then, Aah suppose, everybody in the town got into the habit . . . anything interesting washed ashore just got given to the Watch House. Memorials, like in a church. Everybody likes being remembered, don't they? Even poor drowned buggers a thousand miles from home . . .'

He broke off. 'Aah'd better get *ye* home, else Prudie'll be fretting.'

As they reached the door, Anne gave one last look back. In the dusk at the far end of the room, Arthur's model lighthouse had begun flashing at last.

19

'Run back an' switch it off – there's a good lass. Then turn the key in the lock an' fetch it when you come.' Arthur started towards the cottage, whistling.

Anne suddenly wished Arthur had waited. The rocket-hall was very dark, now the lights were off. She hurried down it with her eyes on the floor. Her footsteps sounded hollow on the bare boards. Hollow and too loud in that private place. But who could be listening?

She pushed the switch over, and the lighthouse stopped flashing.

As she turned back, she made the mistake of looking up. All around her, the twisted dusty blackened gear of foreign dead men hung. Too much of it. Personal, intimate as a seaboot, and old. But even poor drowned buggers wanted to be remembered . . .'

The figureheads watched her, with their white eyes and shattered out-thrust stumps of hands. She had an overpowering feeling they wanted to hold her there; *could* hold her there. She would have to pass each pair of hands and white eyes, all the way to the door. And it seemed a very long way to that door.

She thought for a terrible moment that her legs were not going to move at all, as in a dream. And when she did move, it took her all her will-power not to run.

Once outside, she turned to look back, strangely breathless, but ready to laugh at herself for being a superstitious cow.

Arthur's lighthouse was flashing again.

But she'd switched it off! She knew she had.

She wouldn't have gone back for all the tea in

China. She closed the door firmly, and locked it. Then went and looked through the window.

The lighthouse was dark.

Then it began flashing again.

She was going to have to get used to Arthur's wiring, before it landed her in the funny-farm.

3

Next morning Anne wakened feeling hot and frowsty. Prudie always put too many blankets on, and insisted on closed windows because fresh air became mysteriously evil at sunset.

She jumped up quickly and opened her porthole wide, letting the breeze play through her night-dress as she looked across the river.

It shouldn't have been pretty. The far shore was mainly oil-refinery, and the Gar rolled into the North Sea striped with sewage. But the morning mist pressed the refinery to a flat blue lace, and the morning sun glinted on the sewage like moving jewels. Even the miserable mass of the Middens was alive with gulls, preening, flying in pointless circles, and dive-bombing a gap between their sitting companions as they came in to land. They squabbled over useless bits of seaweed, or set up a hee-hawing kind of squawking, just for the sake of making a noise.

Just like Mother. Anne rolled the thought round her mind, smiling, pleased with it.

There was a tap on the door. Prudie put her head round.

'Miss Anne, whatever are you doing? You'll catch your death at that window. I was going to give you your breakfast in bed, for the first morning.' Her voice had a warm grievance, smothering as the blankets.

Prudie was all set to baby her. This morning was crucial. Whatever happened this morning would set the pattern for the whole holiday, for Prudie was a creature of habit. She must be kept at bay, but not hurt. Talked to in her own language.

'Oh, Prudie, it's such a *lovely* morning. I thought I'd go for a blow. Work up an appetite for breakfast.'

Prudie considered, then nodded. At the crack of dawn, fresh air regained its healing properties. And the chance to get extra food into her darling made up for the lost chance to keep her in bed.

'Wrap up well, then!'

Anne set off down the road, to the bridge across the wagon-way. On her right she could see the little bay, washed free of infant footprints and ice-cream cartons by the morning tide.

On her left, inland, was a shallow valley, full of long, dead grass. The breeze moved the grass in waves. She could see the gusts coming, turning the grass silver in the sun. Silver like a million pointed spearheads pointing at her. Her ears were full of the sound of wind and grass, like surf. As one gust roared past and faded, she could hear the next whispering closer.

She reached the bridge and stood. The railway lines running beneath were orange with rust; the sleepers crumbling to fragments, like cork. Across the rust the briars arched, the bright green of this year tangling through the blackened stems of last. A wagon lay overturned beneath the briars, its wheels the same rusty orange.

Whatever had happened on the wagon-way had happened long ago. Then she understood, for among the briars, lichened blocks of granite lay tilted. Further inland lay stone sheds. This grassy valley had been the stone-yard, when the North Pier was built. The wagon-way had run below Priory cliff to the pier, carrying the granite blocks.

Yard and wagon-way must have been left intact, in case storms damaged the pier. But the pier had been built too well. The wagon-way had crumbled first.

That was OK. Yet ghostly. Anything just left lying for ages must feel ghostly. Like this whole area. The Priory; the Watch House; the little bay that was only lively on sunny days in August... lonely. She searched for the sight of another human being. Only on Priory cliff was a solitary man picking up litter with a pointed stick.

Seaside Garmouth turned its back half a mile up the coast, beyond the Clock Tower. Beyond the grassy valley, industrial Garmouth started, half a mile upriver. Across the river, South Shields was full of factories, houses, buses. But everything was half a mile away. Leaving this place to history, lying under the grass.

How could Prudie stand the loneliness? Perhaps the closed windows and piled-up blankets were meant to keep it out.

Loneliness hit Anne like a knife. It didn't matter that the sun was shining. She closed her eyes to the emptiness of it all. But she couldn't close her ears to the sound of wind: in the grass, on the sea, in the tap of nylon rope on aluminium mast from the beach.

She turned for home. The Watch House watched from its many dark windows.

She realized she was going to have to keep herself very very busy.

When she got back, breakfast was a mountain. Cereal and bacon and two eggs (fresh yesterday, my jewel!). Toast cut half an inch thick; home-made marmalade. Prudie hovered between the washing-up and a cup of coffee on the breakfast-table, watchful as a warder till every last piece was eaten.

Just as Anne felt fit to burst, with two pieces of toast still to go, Arthur arrived. He threw a plaited straw bag on the table with a thump that made the cups rattle.

'Shut your eyes,' he commanded, 'and sniff inside there!'

Anne closed her eyes and sniffed.

'What can ye smell?'

'Nothing.'

'Good,' said Arthur with satisfaction. 'Ye can open your eyes now.' He up-ended the bag, and a mass of fish slithered onto the oilcloth. They gaped at Anne sorrowfully.

'Fish,' said Arthur superfluously. 'But ye couldn't smell nowt, could ye? Cos *fresh* fish has no smell. What you smell in the fish shops is fish a week old; *rotting* fish. Whole country eats rotting fish, 'cept them as knows, in Garmouth.'

'Arthur,' wailed Prudie. 'Ye'll put the bairn off her breakfast.'

25

'I was finished anyway,' said Anne, hastily abandoning the last bits of toast.

'There, what did I tell you!' said Prudie in dark triumph. 'And she was eating hearty till you come. How can I fatten the bairn up, if you go upsetting her like that?'

'Where did all the fish come from?' asked Anne quickly.

'That's me day's fry.'

'He gets it helping out at the Fish Market,' added Prudie.

'From the last catch the boats make before they come to harbour,' added Arthur. 'These fellers were swimming three hours ago.'

'But we can't eat all that,' gasped Anne, 'inside a week.'

'A *week*?' roared Arthur. 'Not on your Nelly. Aah'll have another fresh fry tomorrow.'

Anne closed her eyes and envisaged six weeks eating her way through an endless mountain of fish. But she needn't have worried.

'Orders?' said Arthur briskly.

'Three nice plaice for the grocer. And Mrs McTurk wants a nice fillet of haddock. And that farmer's wife at Cullercoats has cod on Tuesdays . . .'

Arthur took a long broad knife from the table-drawer, and carried the fish to the sink. He chopped and slashed with terrifying speed, pausing only to drink tea from a pint-pot silvered with fish-scales. The ginger cat had placed himself strategically on the draining-board. Every time Arthur turned for another fish, the cat reached out a questing paw, trying to knock a prime fillet on the floor. Arthur kept slamming down his knife on the offending paw. Twenty times Anne's heart was in her mouth; but the cat was always just quick enough to avoid maiming.

'Aah wish they wouldn't *do* that,' said Prudie. 'Three-legged cats is useless for mice.'

In half an hour, the kitchen table resembled a fish-monger's slab, and the fish-heads were boiling on the hob for the cat.

'Do you *give* it away?' asked Anne, amazed.

'No, hinny, norrexactly. One good turn deserves another. Tell the farmer's wife I'd be obliged for a few potatoes, Arthur.'

Anne glanced at the home-made marmalade in front of her, clearly labelled *J. McTurk 1975*.

'D'you buy everything with fish?'

'Not *buy*,' said Prudie, shocked. 'Just friends doing favours like. Garmouth folk will do anything for a nice bit of fish. Mind you, it's no good wi' the Post Office or the Electric, like. We use Arthur's Navy pension for *that lot*.'

Anne pitied the postmaster, eating his solitary rotting fish.

'Aye,' said Arthur. 'Fish comes in handy. Even the bloody government can't take your fish off you.' He departed with his packets carefully wrapped in newspaper.

'What you doing with yourself this morning, Miss Anne?'

'Can I help you, Prudie?'

'Oh no, pet. You're here for a *holiday*. To enjoy yourself, not do housework. Besides, it's all done, bar your breakfast things. Aah can't sleep like Aah used to, so Aah might as well get up early and get done.'

True enough, when Anne got back to her bedroom, the bed was made and all her things tidied away as neatly as a barracks. It was depressing somehow; made her feel homeless.

The best cure for that was to *do* something. She put her Post Office book and the twenty pounds she had managed to extract from Mother in her anorak pocket and set off to explore.

She hadn't gone fifty yards when there was the noise of hoofs and iron rumbling behind. It was Arthur riding a two-wheeled cart pulled by a small fat pony. Arthur's iron toe-plates trailed on the road, making sparks and adding to the din. He pulled up. The cart was bright green; straggly lettering along the side announced *Arthur Purdie, General Dealer. Light Removals*. On the back was the fish.

But it was the pony that interested Anne.

'You want to watch that bugger or he'll nip yer,' said Arthur. 'Look what he done to me jumper.' He opened his reefer-jacket to display a six-inch hole in his maroon pullover, lovingly darned with scarlet wool. 'They're all the same, Gallowers. Bad tempered buggers. He bit a hole in a car-wing once, and Aah had bother wi' the Insurance.' Anne looked at the sly little eyes peering out of the shadow of blinkers, and decided to leave well alone. The Gallower repelled sentiment.

'Aah'll give yer a ride if yer willing to walk,' said Arthur. He dismounted and they walked up the hill together.

'Yer want to watch that feller in the Post Office. He's from London; only been here twenty year.'

Anne glanced down. The blue tip of her Post Office

28

book just protruded from her pocket. Arthur's eyes had lost nothing with age.

'*I'm* a Londoner.'

'Aye, but yer mam's a Garmouth lass, an' it shows. Ye can have a ride now. Just let yer legs dangle.' He gave the Gallower a coarse instruction. The Gallower laid back its ears as primly as a Vicar, and shot like a rocket up Front Street. The flat bed of the cart jarred every bone in Anne's body, and the noise was appalling.

'Lucky I've got a fat bottom,' screamed Anne.

'Aye, this wouldn't suit yer mam.'

They grinned at each other.

But the Gallower had small taste for athletics. After a hundred yards he dropped to a walk. Arthur let him, because he had served his purpose; every head in the street was turning.

'What fettle the day, Arthur?'

'That was a lovely bit of haddock last week.'

'This Miss Fiona's bairn, then?'

'Enjoying your holiday, hinny? Garmouth air'll soon put roses in yer cheeks.'

They were *too* friendly; too cheerful; too ready to pretend she really was on holiday. It was obvious they knew all about Mother's antics. In a minute they would turn away and say 'poor bairn' in that soulful Geordie way she knew so well from Prudie. The harder people tried to be nice, the lonelier Anne felt. Why couldn't Prudie have kept her big mouth shut?

'What cheer, Arthur?'

'What cheer, Fred? How's your Margaret?'

'Fine. Can she have some herrings for grilling on Monday?'

29

'I'll get off here,' said Anne hastily, having shaken hands twenty times in as many yards.

'Dinner's at twelve sharp. Got yer watch? Don't be late or Prudie'll be making buttons.'

She went into a shop to buy a postcard for Daddy.

'You'll be at Prudie's then,' said the thin lady behind the counter. 'Aah mind yer mam well. Prudie used to bring her into this shop every Tuesday to buy Black Bullets.'

Why did it always have to be Mother? Why didn't anyone remember Daddy? But Daddy had been born in Birmingham.

Only the sourfaced Postmaster had nothing to say; obviously he was kept short of gossip as well as fish.

Anne was in a fine stew of miserable loneliness by the time she saw the bicycle. It was a defiant red, and had a huge basket on the handlebars. It was for sale. Ten pounds. Nearly half her money. And she didn't usually ride bicycles; hardly touched her own at home. And it would mean going back to the Post Office, to argue her money back out of the sourfaced Postmaster.

But she suddenly wanted the bike very badly. She could use it to get away from all this; to explore the coast. Most of all, she knew if she bought it, it would infuriate Mother. It was a way of saying she was more than a parcel to be dumped in Garmouth for the summer; it was a way of saying she had a mind of her own.

Into the shop she went.

'You'll be at Prudie's then?' asked the man. 'Aah remember selling your mam a tricycle when she was half your size . . .'

Anne gritted her teeth pleasantly, and felt the tyres. 'It's a good'un,' said the man. 'Five pounds to you.'

'Five?'

'Aye. An' give Arthur a message, will you? Can my missus have halibut on Thursday, 'stead of rock turbot?'

She still had five pounds in her purse; and vowed she would remember about the haddock.

'Halibut, hinny,' said the man patiently, as to a backward child. 'Halibut instead of rock turbot.'

She bought apples from a woman who remembered Mother buying apples, and cycled back to the end of Front Street, where the ruins stood on their cliff. It would be a good place to eat apples and think. The ruins turned out to be Garmouth Priory, *Department of the Environment. Admission: Adults 10p Children 5p. Special terms for parties of twenty or more.* The lovely curator didn't know her from Adam.

'You still at school? Five pence!'

She looked at the array of guidebooks and postcards.

'Doing a project, are you? Project for school?' He seemed so eager she hadn't the heart to disillusion him. It must be lonely picking up litter with a stick all day.

'Well, the first thing to remember is that three kings are buried here. That's why there's three crowns on the town crest. King Oswin, who was done in by his brother; King Malcolm who was done in near Alnwick (he was seven feet tall) and a king Aah can never remember who was done in by his subjects when he came back from exile . . . it's a lovely

31

graveyard. An' Aah'll tell ye who's buried here an' all . . . Alexander Rollo!'

'Oh, yes?' said Anne cautiously.

'You must remember Alexander Rollo?'

'Er, no.'

'He held the lantern at the burial of Sir John Moore at Corunna – that's in Spain. Sir John Moore and Alexander Rollo was fighting Napoleon. Surely you've learned the poem in school?'

'Er, no.'

'I don't knaa what they teach bairns these days.' The man took a stance, left-hand thumb in waistcoat pocket, right hand extended.

> 'Not a drum was heard, not a funeral note,
> As his corpse to the rampart we hurried;
> Not a soldier discharged his farewell shot
> O'er the grave where our hero we buried.
>
> 'We buried him darkly at dead of night,
> The sods with our bayonets turning,
> By the struggling moonbeam's misty light
> And the lanthorn dimly burning.'

The curator paused and said, 'That was the lantern that Alexander Rollo was holding, see?'

'Yes,' said Anne, a little embarrassed because a crowd was gathering. Well, three people anyway. But the curator was plunging on.

> 'Few and short were the prayers we said,
> And we spoke not a word of sorrow

32

*But we steadfastly looked on the face that was
  dead
And we bitterly thought of the morrow.'*

The curator paused again. There was a little sound of clapping, and an American voice said, 'Is this part of the *regular* service?'

The curator, suddenly aware of other duties, waved Anne through the Priory gate with a grand gesture.

'Enjoy yourself – a lovely graveyard. Only,' he added darkly, 'if ye see a dog hanging aboot . . . a scruffy-looking object . . . throw a brick at it for me.'

'*Brick*?' Anne was, in an instant, all indignant animal-lover.

'Aye. It's a bad bugger. Always hanging roond. Some of the old tombs is not very secure, see? Aah've seen that brute wi' a human shinbone in its mouth afore now.'

4

It *was* a lovely graveyard, oddly enough. All the tombstones were over a hundred years old, and the north-east gales had weathered their lettering into strange whirling shapes that were impossible to read close-to. But if you stood well back, ghostly names jumped out at you suddenly. And there was soft turf, and the blue horizon. A warm breath of wind and the distant sound of waves at the foot of the cliff.

She found Corporal Alexander Rollo, late of the Royal Artillery. He cheered her up no end, because he had died peacefully at the great age of eighty-two, with his children and grandchildren around him. The great Sir John Moore had perished, but little Corporal Rollo had survived, despite his sorrowful thoughts of the morrow.

She sat leaning against his tombstone, chewing an apple and writing to Daddy. After all, she was only two hundred miles from home, not two thousand like Corporal Rollo.

Dear Daddy,

I am sending this to the Works. Are you sleeping in your office again? Will you please write and tell me what is happening? I am with Prudie at Brigade Cottage, Garmouth. She hasn't changed a bit. I bought a bike for five pounds this morning. What is happening about Toby? Love Anne.

Then, as an afterthought, she scrawled *I didn't want to leave with mother*, right up the side of the card. It made the card look terrible. But she left it. It was what she felt.

She also felt very miserable when she'd finished. When she had posted the card she would have nothing else left to do. She couldn't think of any plans at all. She didn't want to talk to any more strangers, because it was exhausting. But she didn't want to be alone because it was lonely. She looked at her watch. Half past ten. Ninety minutes to lunch. She didn't dare go back before, or Prudie would fret. Miss Anne was supposed to be on holiday, *enjoying* herself.

She was just on the point of collapsing into a slobbering lump when she saw something grey moving between the tombstones. It was low, like a dog.

Glad of something to do, she gave chase. But it was elusive, dodging and turning. And there were so many gravestones: ranks of them; streets of them.

Then suddenly she cornered it, by the cliff's edge. It was a wretched thing, thin, with no collar. She felt a wave of sympathy; it was lost, as she was. She wouldn't throw bricks, she'd make friends. Bring it scraps. Of fish. Especially of fish.

It was backing into a narrow gap between two leaning box-tombs. She approached it correctly, crouching down, offering it a hand to smell, palm upwards, near the ground. She was good with dogs; Daddy had taught her.

The dog had retreated into a kind of cave it had scrabbled out under one of the tombs. It was bald in patches, and ribs showed through the bare grey skin. People could be so cruel to dogs . . .

It sniffed her hand and relaxed. Stopped shivering. It began to worm its way towards her, on its elbows, belly to the ground. Then it looked up into her face and snarled. Its teeth were old and yellow.

It snarled again. Not in fear; in deliberate malice. She suddenly felt nervous, crouched in the narrow space between the tombs. She backed away and it followed, still snarling, the black of its lips moving back and forwards across the yellow teeth. Eyes watching her as no dog's had ever watched before.

She regained the open air and straightened up. She suddenly hated the dog; loathed it. She looked round for a stone to throw; pulled a cracked piece off a tomb at the risk of her fingernails.

But when she turned, the dog was gone.

She put back the cracked piece of tomb, very ashamed of herself. Whatever had got into her? It was only a lost dog. She was getting hysterical. She must get back among people, even if they were strangers. Huh, you fool, she said to herself. And shook herself and tried to laugh, only to find she couldn't stop her silly breathless panting.

She couldn't stop herself looking over her shoulder, all the way to the gatehouse.

She didn't quite reach the gate, however, because she almost fell over a most reassuring sight.

Two young clergymen lay on the turf that sloped to the river, sheltered from the wind by tombstones and getting the best of the sun. They had taken off the coats of their grey clerical suits; white shirts showed behind their black clerical-fronts.

One was short and tubby, with dark curly hair

balding in front. The other was tall and fair and incredibly good-looking.

'The main trouble with this town,' said the fair one, 'is a total lack of *sin*.'

'Amendment, Father. A total lack of *interesting* sin.'

'Agreed, Father. They get drunk twice a week.'

'And beat their wives.'

'Though they would never have *dreamt* of doing so, if they hadn't had a drop too much to drink.'

'They knock off scrap brass from Smith's Dock. But they don't think that's worth confessing at all.'

'Confessions? I'm lucky if I hear one a week. And that's some old budgie from the Mothers' Union, confessing to uncharitable thoughts because her friend got more currants in her bun.'

'Where's the *lust*?'

'Where's the *vice*?'

'Only in the pages of the *News of the World*.'

'Can you imagine an orgy in Garmouth?'

'Waste of good drinking-time.'

Anne didn't really mean to eavesdrop, but the conversation was so fascinating. She crouched behind a tombstone.

'Mrs Thomas is knitting me another pair of socks, Father.'

'Mrs O'Malley has knitted me another scarf.'

'That's a vice – scarf-knitting.'

'Not in the Holy Rule-Book, Father. You can't rule a woman offside for knitting scarves.'

'I shall die of boredom before I finish this curacy.'

'I've got two more curacies to go. That's the Church of Rome for you.'

'You signed up for the wrong team, Father.'

'You offering a transfer-fee?'

'Your team draws the big gates.' The tall curate stretched and yawned luxuriously. 'I know what I shall do. I shall write an avant-garde book, like the Bishop of Woolwich. But what *about*? It's all been done.'

'Trace the homosexual influences in the Highway Code?'

'God, sex and Brownies?'

Anne leaned over the tombstone for a better look. Unfortunately, the tombstone leaned with her. She rolled down the slope in a minor avalanche of soil and landed at their feet.

'We have a visitation, Father.'

'Heavenly or demonic?'

'Earthly, I think. Certainly *earthy*.'

'I'm terribly sorry,' said Anne, brushing herself off and blushing furiously. 'I was eavesdropping.'

'Compliments will get you everywhere,' said the tall curate. 'Let me introduce us. I am Father Fletcher of the High Church of England, and this is Father da Souza of the Church of Rome. As you will have gathered from his accent, he is an ambassador to our shores. One day he will hatch out as the first All-American Pope. After I have passed on to my reward, I hope.'

'Are you a Catholic?' asked Father da Souza kindly.

'Canvassing again,' said Father Fletcher. 'I wonder Rome doesn't buy TV advertising slots . . .'

'Seeing how much harm that's done the Church of England . . .'

Anne wriggled uncomfortably. 'I'm not a Catholic. I suppose I'm nothing, really.'

'The Church of England lays claim to all nothing-reallies,' said Father Fletcher.

'But,' said Anne, determined to get a word in edgeways, 'I'm interested in Quakers and Buddhists.'

'A kind of religious vegetable-salad,' said Father Fletcher.

'Why Quakers and Buddhists?' asked Father da Souza.

'Because they don't compel people to join their faith by *force*,' said Anne blushing again.

'Oh deary me,' said Father Fletcher, laughing fit to burst. 'She has you there, friend of Rome.'

'Canterbury burnt martyrs, too,' snapped da Souza. Then he turned to Anne with serious eyes. 'Can we help you in any way?'

'We can help her put the tombstone back,' said Father Fletcher. 'We don't want the dear departed having an identity-crisis.'

'Shut up, Father. I'm serious.' He looked at Anne with such a quiet waiting, that she found herself talking before she knew it. She told him about being sent to stay with Arthur and Prudie. She nearly told him why; he had a way of drawing things out of you. But she drew back from trying to explain about Daddy and Mother and Uncle Monty. She told him about the dog instead.

Da Souza stared at the ground, pulling out tiny blades of grass with deep concentration. 'I don't like the sound of that dog. I wonder we haven't seen it; we come here often enough.'

'We must dog its footsteps,' said Father Fletcher. But his laugh failed under his friend's look.

'This graveyard's typical of the whole Church of England. What is it? A holy place or a public park? Children playing football; courting couples – it's not even respected as an ancient monument.'

'Oh c'mon. I've seen plenty of neglected graveyards in Italy.'

'Neglected but respected. Here, it's ridiculous. If a man robbed these graves of bones, he'd be put in prison. But a dog can do it with impunity. Nobody even bothers to ask who the dog belongs to.'

'You must excuse my friend,' said Father Fletcher. 'Being American, he takes everything seriously.'

'And you make everything a joke!' For a second there was a feel of real needle in the air. Then da Souza smiled and said, 'I've never been inside the Watch House, more's the shame. Sounds interesting. We must come and see it.'

'Yes,' said Anne solemnly, hiding a suddenly light heart. Father Fletcher was nice in his way, but she'd never met anyone like Father da Souza before.

'We have a youth club at the parish church,' broke in Father Fletcher. 'Wednesday night and Saturday night. Only the usual square scene – table-tennis and cut-price Coke. But they're a friendly lot. Think there's a disco this Saturday. Why don't you look in?'

'Thank you,' said Anne, in a polite voice that meant she wouldn't. Didn't he know that for solitary girls youth clubs were a blood sport?

'Must be off,' said Father Fletcher. 'Lunch at

twelve. My superior-in-God's wife's usual – cold fat lamb and high thinking.'

'You ought to try Mrs O'Malley's stew. It would un-nerve St Ignatius Loyola. Ah, well, what we suffer in this world . . .'

5

The rain drumming on the roof wakened her. She looked at her watch. Seven a.m. She'd planned this morning so carefully. Early walk. Breakfast. Cycle to the Public Library. Then a good read till lunch, leaning against Corporal Rollo's tombstone. Keeping busy and out of Prudie's way.

But the drumming of the rain ruined everything. She turned over in a mood of cosy despair and went back to sleep.

The gentle shaking of Prudie's hand wakened her.

'Aah've brought your breakfast, Miss Anne. It's a terrible morning. Arthur's come in like a drooned rat. Aah had to sit and dry his hair, afore he caught his death. He ought to have more sense at his age, gone seventy. But it's no good telling him.' She bustled off, full of aggrieved triumph.

Anne ate her breakfast slowly. Actually, it *was* nice being fussed over. Like the time she'd had measles, when she was seven. Big fire in the nursery and Prudie doing the ironing, singing made-up words to the music on the radio . . .

But that reminded her of Daddy, alone. Toby alone in some rotten stables where they didn't care. Mother with Monty . . .

If she stayed in bed one minute more, she'd go stark raving bonkers.

'Oh, pardon *me*.' Prudie, coming in for the break-fast-tray without knocking, found Anne standing stark naked, wondering what to wear. Prudie turned her back abruptly and began tidying the dressing-table, her neck pink with embarrassment. Naked six-year-olds were her stock-in-trade, but Anne had turned decidedly female since then. 'I thought I'd let you have a lie-in this morning, for a treat. There's nothing to get up for really.'

'*I'll* make the bed,' said Anne stubbornly.

'No, hinny, leave it,' said Prudie even more stub-bornly. 'You're on your holidays.'

The bathroom was tiny. Full of green light like an underwater telephone-kiosk. The highly polished taps shone like sad goldfish. The drumming on the roof was so loud it got inside Anne's head. What was she going to do all day?

The living room wasn't much bigger; not with Arthur installed in one corner, moodily plaiting a decorative knot from thick string.

'Aye,' he said, partly a greeting and partly a sigh. His newly-dried hair was fluffing up all around his head.

'Is it going to get out?' asked Anne, proud at remembering the Geordie phrase.

'Going to get worse,' said Arthur. 'Glass is falling. Looks set in for the day.'

Through the window, Anne could see the Gar running ten-foot waves: white triangles of foam speeding along the South Pier as fast as motorcars.

'Fancy your hand at knotting?' asked Arthur companionably.

'Mmm,' said Anne.

'Have some sense, Arthur,' said Prudie. 'What interest would Miss Anne have in *knotting*? Knotting's a man's thing.'

'She *said* she did,' roared Arthur.

Both the old people looked at her expectantly.

'Excuse me – I must get something from my room,' said Anne, and fled. She timed three minutes carefully by her watch, then went back. Prudie had won the muttered argument. The thick string was nowhere to be seen; and Arthur was tapping the barometer in the hall with a certain desperation.

'Aah've put you some books out,' said Prudie. Anne looked at them; they were the kind Prudie always read. Each had a girl on the front cover, staring up into the eyes of a straight-nosed, impossibly-handsome man. Sometimes the girl wore nurse's uniform; sometimes riding-jodhpurs. Sometimes she was blonde and sometimes brunette. But it was the same girl, and she always succumbed to the same fate. Love, misunderstanding, neglect; a meeting with another man who turned out to be a rotter. Reconciliation and wedding-bells.

Anne picked up the first and began to read. The only way to stay sane was to fantasize. The first girl was called Rosalind. She was private secretary to a brain-surgeon. Anne had her in bed with the surgeon by page five; aborted by page twenty and on main-line heroin by page thirty.

'I wish you'd stop fussing about and get from under my feet, Arthur!'

Anne heard Arthur thump down into his rocking-chair; the legs creaked in protest.

On page forty-five, the brain-surgeon had an affair

with a nubile pair of Siamese twins. On page fifty he had a nervous breakdown.

Arthur began to rock and whistle a tune.

'Shush, Arthur. Not in front of Miss Anne. That's not a nice tune at *all*.'

The brain-surgeon had his breakdown because both Siamese twins had to have abortions.

Arthur began drawing on his pipe, which made horrible bubbling noises.

'*Arthur!*'

'What's up with you, woman? Miss Anne don't mind a bit of smoking,' roared Arthur. 'Do you, Miss Anne?' Anne could tell from his tone of outrage that he would have been allowed to smoke if she hadn't been there.

Again, both the old people were looking at her expectantly. And she couldn't walk out again. She couldn't retreat to her bedroom to read, or Prudie would think she was offended or brooding, and be at the bedroom door every five minutes with a cup of tea and an offer of aspirin.

And still the rain beat on the windows, a thick streaming green.

Then she had the bright idea.

'Arthur?' Her tone was childishly enquiring.

'Yes, my jewel?'

'Who dusts all the things in the Watch House?'

'You might well ask,' said Prudie. 'They don't see a duster from one year's end to the next. Aah've offered many a time. But no; Aah might break something that's beyond a mere *woman's* understanding. And if this feller and his cronies has a spare minute from playing Guy Fawkes wi' them rockets, they're

45

on that billiard-table. They'll end up looking like billiard-balls.'

'Can I dust the things for you, Arthur?'

Arthur twinkled with glee. 'Course you can, my jewel. Clever girl like you knows what to dust wi'out breaking things.'

'Huh,' said Prudie. 'Lot of old rubbish. Shoulda been put in the bin years ago.'

But she knew she was beaten. She returned with two spotless dusters.

'Wrap up well, chick. That place is as cold as charity.'

'By,' said Arthur, 'this key's stiff. Hasn't been turned in my time as caretaker.'

They were standing in the wind-thrummed silence of the billiard-room, which led off the far end of the rocket-hall. The billiard-table stood under its sheet like an eight-legged elephant. A notice on the overhead light said *Please do not smoke while playing at the table*. The walls were lined with racks for billiard-cues and benches for spectators. There was a rack of white clay pipes variously labelled *Billy Jim* and *The Bosun* and *Wee Tich*. These obviously belonged to Arthur's old cronies.

But it wasn't just a billiard-room. The sea of maritime curios that nearly flooded the rocket-hall had seeped in here too. There was a small brass cannon in the fire-place. There was a framed press-cutting about a rocket-rescue off the Norwegian coast in 1937, and the first photograph taken under-water of a deep-sea diver at work.

But most of the curios were confined to a row of

glass cabinets. They lined one whole wall, from floor to ceiling; brown woodwork blistered with years of sun.

It was with the key of the first of these cabinets that Arthur had been struggling. The key turned gratingly at last.

'Looka this, then! These are the identical plates used by Bobby Shaftoe when he dined at Beamish Hall. That's in County Durham. It's a museum now.'

'Bobby Shaftoe?'

'Haven't ye heard o' Bobby Shaftoe?' Arthur's voice had the outrage of a pop-fan discovering someone who hasn't heard of the Beatles.

'I just didn't know he was a real person, that's all.'

> *'Bobby Shaftoe's gyen to sea*
> *Silver buckles on his knee*
> *He'll come back and marry me*
> *Bonny Bobby Shaftoe,'*

Arthur sang, beating time with something he'd picked off the shelf. 'Have you never sung that at school?'

'Oh, yes,' said Anne. But her eyes were on the thing that Arthur was beating time with. It was a human jawbone, with all the front teeth missing. Arthur followed her eyes.

'Aye, it's always the same. It's a feller's front teeth always go first.' He pointed to the shelf above the Shaftoe plates. There was a whole row of jawbones: some grey, some a dark, varnished toffee-brown.

'The grey ones were dug up by fellers from Durham University. Out on the Priory graveyard. Them's

47

monks. The dark ones was picked up by fishermen on the Black Middens. Them's sailors.' He returned the jaw to its place. 'Ye can manage, then? Lock up when ye've finished. There's some valuable things in these cabinets.'

He made sure the other keys would open the other cabinets and left, whistling. Now he could sit with Prudie and smoke and make knots in peace. But Anne wondered whether peace can be too dearly bought, as she surveyed the jawbones and the whole skull that lay with them. Of course she'd touched a skeleton in the biology lab at school. But that was covered with plastic labels saying *cranium* and *clavicle*. Besides, the other girls had been there. These jaws were parts of real people: monks and sailors.

A sudden rattle of rain on the windows made her jump. It was either start or run away. And if she didn't start with the jaws, she'd never do them. She tried poking at them with a corner of the duster. But that would have taken for ever.

She picked up the first jaw. It felt dry, light and cold. She said 'excuse me' to the late owner and dusted the molars in a vigorous no-nonsense manner. She wiped the shelf underneath and put the jaw back.

Well, that hadn't been very terrible. She did the other five briskly. Then the skull. Soon they were all sitting back on a shining shelf. They didn't seem to mind at all.

After that, the Shaftoe plates were a walk-over. They had brown hunting-and-fishing scenes; quite interesting.

She had to get a chair to do the next shelf up. It held a rack of dark broken clay-pipes, picked up by fishermen on the Middens. But there *was* something odd . . .

Someone had written in the thick dust, on the shelf in front of the pipes. Big childish lettering. It was too dark to read.

She went and put the billiard-room lights on. One of them glowed steadily, but the other one kept flickering. The nearest one, damn it.

She spelled out the letters. H . . . E . . . L. And another letter that hadn't been finished for lack of room. It could have been another L.

HELL.

Kids messing about. Years ago. When kids got a big kick from writing *hell* in all sorts of places. Now they had to write words like *shit* or worse to get any kick at all. As Mother would have, said, *hell* was old hat. Anne grinned and swept off the lettering with one flick of the duster. She caught a corner of the pipe-rack and all the pipes rattled drily.

The next shelf was so high she couldn't see on to it even with a chair. She didn't feel like reaching into it blind; it could have held *anything*. Come back later with a ladder, when Arthur was there to help . . .

Coward, she thought with a grin. She polished the glass door, inside and out, and stepped back to admire her handiwork. The jaws grinned back; they seemed quite pleased. To a dentist they'd be all in a day's work.

The next case was full of silver cruets and ladles in velvet cases. *From the steamship* STANLEY *wrecked on the Middens 24th November 1874. Presented with gratitude to Garmouth Life Brigade by the Captain.* At least one captain hadn't gone down with his ship.

There was more writing in the dust on the shelf. A . . . N. Somebody's initials? And there was *Hel* again. With another letter. A? Y? No, a P. *Help*?

She swept it away quickly, so she wouldn't have to think about it.

But there it was again, in the next case. A.N.HELP. The writing was bigger, wilder, more urgent. It was beginning to get on her nerves.

Another sudden gust of rain rattled on the windows, and this time she not only jumped, but broke out all over in a tingling sweat. So that was what writers meant by 'a cold sweat'?

Get hold of yourself, girl. Graffiti are everywhere. She'd read a book about it once. The book said all the best ones started in New York. There were some very funny ones. *Help feed my hobbit. Make peace or I'll kill ya!*

They didn't seem so funny now.

Another shelf. A.N.A.N.A.N. A.N.A.N.A.N She wished they would stop. One more case, then she'd go and have lunch. She began to hurry, as if she was in a race. The dust flew in clouds, making her cough.

She moved up her chair to the last glass case. She looked inside. More writing.

But it was moving! Balls of fluff being pushed around like tiny mice. More letters appeared as she watched.

ANHELPANHELPANHELP

Anne Help.

Inside a glass case that hadn't been opened in Arthur's time. She stuck her knuckles in her mouth and bit them hard. She didn't even notice the noises coming out of her own mouth.

The writing stopped.

She never knew how she got outside. Only that she was standing in the pouring rain with the keys in her hand and Prudie rushing out of the cottage door towards her, calling.

'Miss Anne, Miss Anne, what's the matter? You'll catch pneumonia standing like that!'

Then she fainted.

6

Ammonia spearing up her nose.

'S'all right,' she heard Arthur say. 'Steady wi' the smelling salts. Here she comes now.'

'I'll fetch her a dose of sal volatile,' said Prudie in a voice that implied she wasn't accepting good news *that* quickly.

'Writing,' said Anne. 'Writing in the dust, behind the glass.'

'What?' said Arthur. 'Big childish scribbling like? Is that what scared ye?'

Anne opened her eyes and nodded.

Arthur cackled, a comforting sound. The real world came back in focus. 'That's the Old Feller . . .'

But Prudie wasn't comforted. She exploded.

'If you say one more thing, Arthur Purdie, Aah'm leaving this house and Aah'm leaving you. Putting ideas like that in the bairn's head, the state she's in. One more word, Aah said, an' ye can do your own washing and ironing!'

'All right, stop making buttons, woman. The lights is still on in the Watch House. Aah'll go and turn them off.' He departed in a moderate huff.

'What did he mean, the Old Feller?' asked Anne.

'Nowt,' said Prudie, 'and less than nowt. Let the old fools do their own dusting.'

But Anne could hear the jumpiness in her voice.

It took all afternoon to soothe Prudie down; all the afternoon with Anne swallowing this and that against pneumonia, and having to lie down on the couch and read dreary love-stories. She had a handsome country vet shot by the Mafia, in the middle of saving the heroine's horse. She made a rising young cabinet minister go on a Jack the Ripper rampage. But the game soon palled.

Peace only returned when Prudie departed, in her best hat, for the Garmouth Women's Happy Hour at the Non-Conformist chapel. Arthur was sitting in his rocker with the local paper, looking oddly scholarly in his reading-spectacles.

'Arthur?'

'Aye?' he said, non-committally.

'Tell me about the Old Feller!'

'Ye'll get me shot,' said Arthur in tones of enjoyable terror. 'Not a word to Prudie, then?'

'Not a word.'

Arthur nodded, satisfied. 'Well, it's daft, really, when you come to think of it. The Watch House is always full of little noises. Bound to be, made of wood. After a hot day or rain, the planks shift while they're settling down. It can sound like footsteps, and we say 'The Old Feller's restless tonight'. For a laugh, like.

'And things get moved round. Stands to reason. In a storm the whole cliff shakes when the waves hit it. Spray comes right over the Watch House. Things get knocked over. Or sometimes they get just edged to the point of falling when the storm stops. They're just left hanging there by a hair's breadth. Then the sun comes out an' the planks shift, and the thing

53

that's just hanging falls wi' a great rattle in the quiet. It can be a bit jumpy Aah suppose – Prudie doesn't like it – but we just shrug and say it's the Old Feller. Aah don't know why. When Aah joined the Brigade, all the old'uns used to say it. And you know how young'uns copy old'uns? Ye could call it a joke that's lasted seventy years – daft really.'

'You mean he's just a saying – not a real person?'

'Oh, he was real, all right. A little old man who gave his whole life to the Brigade. There was nothing he wouldn't do – flag-day collecting – anything. Never missed a call when a ship was in distress. Then he got a dickey heart an' the doctor said he couldn't do it no more.

'But one night there was a big wreck. All the lads were busy, and when they got back they found the Old Feller lying dead in the billiard-room. He'd answered his last call, poor little soul. Not a bad way to go, when you think of it. Anyway, even if he does walk and knock things over, he's entitled. He means no harm to the Brigade, that's for sure. He was a canny little feller, Aah believe – everybody's favourite. But it's all a joke really.'

'What about the writing?'

'That's the lads – anything for a laugh. Some of the things Aah've seen written! Once it was *Arthur Purdie, sweet seventeen an' never been kissed*. But the young ones has no imagination. They just write things like *Newcastle United Rule, OK?* or *This shelf is dirty*.' Arthur mourned the passing of old times.

Anne was silent, remembering the balls of fluff. Could they have been moving in a draught? AN HELP . . . AN HELP. Had she imagined it?

54

'Aah hope Aah hasn't upset you, Miss Anne?'

'No – I couldn't worry about the Old Feller now if I *tried*. He sounds *sweet*. I'll go on dusting tomorrow.'

'Ye'll have to settle wi' Prudie first,' said Arthur.

'*Could* you turn your radio down just a bit more, Miss Anne? I don't *mind* that jazzy music, but it does get on your nerves after a bit.'

Anne had spent the last hour wearing Prudie's patience down. Not by doing anything really awful; just one damn thing after another.

Outside, the rain still teemed down, blurring the South Pier. Anne said brightly, 'Arthur's in the Watch House.'

'Aye,' said Prudie. 'Fiddling wi' that dynamo thing for the searchlight. He'll blow us up one of these fine days. Aye, well, that'll be the end of all our troubles.'

'Shall I go and see if he wants coffee?'

'He's not long finished his breakfast. But he's got a crop for all corn, that one. Be as fat as a barrel, if he wasn't on the go all the time. Take him a coffee. Would you like to go and have yours with him? Then I can get Hoovered out.'

Raindrops splashing in the coffee-cups. The Watch House door swinging open, key in the lock. Steady girl. Afraid of the ghost of a poor old man? A canny little soul?

'Arthur?' Her voice ascended the scale shrilly.

There was a vicious buzzing overhead that made her jump. But it was just the electric meter, and the junction-boxes for the searchlight.

'Aah'm here, chick. Come up.'

She climbed the stairs; dark engravings on the walls. Newcastle in flames, 1750, as viewed from the river. The Garmouth lifeboat, struggling through waves that turned and twisted round it like boa-constrictors. A ship aground on sandbanks, under a blue moon; the dark shore thick with rockets and scurrying figures. One of them wore a long white coat . . .

'Up here,' shouted Arthur. She went into a door marked *Crew Room*. It seemed full of men; but it was only rows of black oilskins with sou'westers hung above, and rows of wellingtons below. A ladder went up through the ceiling, with only a rope handrail. She had an awful job with the coffees.

'That's the stuff to give the troops.' Arthur wiped his mouth with the back of his hand, and tipped back the peak of his cap, all in one gesture. They sipped coffee peacefully.

'There's the Thor-Sorensen ferry on her way in,' said Arthur, jerking his thumb at a dim blur between the piers. 'Shall we say good morning?'

'How?'

'Searchlight,' said Arthur, slapping a great black cylinder on a trolley. 'Came off a battlecruiser, afore the First World War. Made a rare difference to the Brigade – we could see what we were shooting rockets at.'

He leapt up, eager as a boy, and swung the cylinder, his eye to a telescopic sight with a perished rubber eyepiece. He thumped down a switch, and a solid beam of light lanced through the rain. Then he pulled a lever, there was a *clack*, and the beam vanished. *Clack*, and it reappeared.

'Morse code,' said Arthur. 'Good morning.' *Clack; clack-clack; clack-clack-clack.* 'Wonder if he'll answer.'

From the grey blur came a pin-point reply.

'There!' said Arthur. 'Shouldn't ha' done it really – misuse of Brigade property. But Aah thought it would interest you. Nice of him to reply, but Aah'm not surprised. They think a lot of the Brigade, do the Norwegians – all sailors do. They know we're here.'

Anne went round and peered in the front of the searchlight.

'Hang on,' said Arthur. 'I'll switch it off at the mains. I don't want an accident while you're looking in. This thing could blind you for life – fry your eyeballs like eggs.'

'Ooh,' said Anne. She could see, far behind the Morse-code shutters, an image of her own face in a mirror: upside-down and queerly distorted. At least she assumed it was her own face. As she stupidly tried to turn her head upside down, the image turned with her.

She waved a hand; the image waved back. At least it had hair the right colour.

Anne kept her dusting to the rocket-room. It was nearer the stairs where Arthur buzzed and clicked. She wasn't quite ready to face the billiard-room's glass cabinets next door.

The rocket-room had a line of model ships. Some were huge models from the shipbuilders, with rows of brass portholes and every piece of rigging perfect. They were easy – just wipe over the glass case. It was the home-made models that took the time: poking between the sails with a sharp corner of the duster. She could see why they weren't dusted often.

One had a name-card in Arthur's straggly writing. *The Famous*

You *couldn't* call a ship *The Famous*! She snatched the card down; it had curled up with time and sun. Opened-out, it read *The Famous* BOUNTY. The model was small and smothered in brown paint, whiskery with fluff down the edges; even Captain Bligh couldn't have loved it. Anne sighed; Arthur was hopeless. Such a jumble of rubbish and wonders; no wonder he had so few visitors.

She turned to the pictures on the walls. Yellowing photographs of ships stuck on the Middens the morning after. Some ships whole, just tilted and slightly ridiculous. Others ghastly tangles of rope and spars.

Then a photo of the Brigade in 1905, a hundred strong, resplendent in caps and moss-stitched ganzies, and white belts lettered GVLB. Garmouth Volunteer Life Brigade.

She bet there weren't a hundred members now.

Then paintings. *Royal Academy 1882*. A great bearded man facing out the storm with proud look and broad ganzied chest. He had a scroll in his clenched hand, carrying the single word *Mercy*. Didn't the Victorian painters lay things on with a trowel?

Portrait followed portrait. She wondered if any of them was of the Old Feller. She didn't think so; they all looked so big and smug.

Then, tucked in a corner, she came across a tinted photograph. She was immediately sure it was the Old Feller. He looked like a ghost even in life. A waif's face, the whole lower half covered in minutely-curling white whiskers, in which his lips floated like painted rosebuds. Old. The windows of the photographer's studio were reflected in his eyes, so you couldn't read his expression.

He wore a cork life-jacket. But it was a studio photo all right, because he was wearing his best Sunday-suit underneath. The louring storm-clouds were clearly painted on canvas, even if the photographer had put them out-of-focus deliberately.

But it was the hands that took her eye. One hooked round the cork life-jacket; the other resting on a plaster rock. Both clenched so tight with tension that Anne clenched her own in sympathy. AN HELP ... AN HELP ... He had to be the one.

There was a crash of broken glass from the billiard-room next door. She ran through unthinking. It was too catastrophically-human a sound to be scared of.

On the covered billiard-table, like an obscene billiard-ball, the skull from the glass case rocked upside down, to and fro. The glass of the case was shattered. The jawbones still stood in their neat row.

She picked up the skull instinctively, puzzled about what had happened. What a heavy skull it was. Much thicker bones than her own; a massive man's skull. She kept rubbing her hands over it, thinking how big the man must have been. It was a horrible feeling that grew and grew, yet she couldn't stop doing it.

'Lord love yer, what's happened?' It was Arthur, all of a fluster. He took the skull from her and peered at it; she saw his mouth tighten, as if he had put his hand on something slightly unpleasant, like a frog. Perhaps he was getting the same feeling of nasty bigness from it.

59

Then he put the skull back in its place, through the shattered glass, without bothering to unlock the cabinet.

'Ah well,' he said, bending down to pick up bits of glass from the floor. 'Worse things happen at sea.' The mottled hands picking up the glass were trembling. 'Don't you fret, Miss Anne; weren't your fault. You were just trying to help. I've got a nice bit of window-pane over at home that'll fit this case nicely. Aah'll do it straight away. Can't stand seeing things lying broken.'

Anne just stared; he was talking nonsense.

All the broken glass lay on the floor; none inside the locked cabinet.

Which could only mean . . .

Arthur went on picking up glass. He never looked at her, and the quaver in his voice showed all his seventy years. He knew more than he was saying. But something told her not to pursue the matter.

She went back to the cottage with him, while he fetched glass and putty. Then she returned to her dusting, while he shaped the new glass with a cutter. The sound set her teeth on edge.

She looked up at the photograph of the Old Feller. It certainly wasn't his skull; his bones were as frail as a chicken's.

Then she paused, cloth raised. In the oily yellow dust that gathers on any uncleaned glass had been written:

An help pleas.

It hadn't been there before.

PART TWO

Twist thou and twine, in light and gloom
A spell is on thy hand,
The wind shall be thy changeful loom,
Thy web the shifting sand.

Twine from this hour, in ceaseless toil,
On Blackrock's sullen shore
Till cordage of the sand shall coil
Where crested surges roar.

R. S. Hawker

7

Arthur looked up from his lunchtime paper. 'Sky's clearing. Be fine this afternoon. Aah'd better inspect the cliff after the rain. Coming for a look?'

Anne frowned. What was so special about a cliff after rain? Was Arthur scared to go back to the Watch House as well?

But as soon as they started to descend the cliff, she saw what Arthur was so worried about. There was a stair down to the Black Middens, at a shallower place in the cliff about fifty yards upriver. Made of packed earth held back with pegged planks.

Or rather, there had been a stair. But the earth had swollen with the rain, and forced the pegs out of place. The planks were lying any-old-how, amidst pools of smooth bluish mud and little landslides of soil. It looked downright dangerous. They slithered down hand-in-hand.

When they reached the bottom, she saw what was so special about Watch House Cliff. It was eighty feet high, but only made of chocolate-brown soil, with a few large white stones set in. The rain had gouged great slimy gullies out of it; a whole network of gullies, like the Mississippi Delta. Worse, between the gullies, huge pinnacles of soil, with grass on top, hung away from the cliff, networked with inch-wide cracks and ready to fall.

'Aah'll have to fence that off an' put up a notice,' said Arthur gloomily.

The rocks at the foot of the cliff were buried in loose soil, like a garden. Arthur kicked the soil. 'Tide'll wash all this away tonight. The rain brings it down and the tide carts it away. This bloody cliff'll finish the Watch House, and finish Prudie an' me an' all. We'll end up in the Workhouse.'

'But the Watch House is ten yards back from the edge!'

'What's ten yards?' He turned her with unusual roughness to look at the river. 'When Aah was a little lad, there was a whole field between the Watch House and the river. The Brigade grazed its horses there. Now where is it? Down on the Middens and away out to sea. What's ten yards? Two year at most.'

'But someone's shoring it up with planks!'

'Aye – me and the lads. And now it's all to do again. Shoring up this cliff wi' planks is like feeding an elephant strawberries.'

'Can't the Council do anything?'

'They nearly did – new sea-wall.' Arthur pointed up-river. A smooth snake of concrete ran along the shore. It ended fifty yards from where they stood, with a tangle of rusting reinforcing-wires poking upwards into the sky.

'Aren't they going to finish it?'

'There's a financial crisis, isn't there? County Council's got cold feet because some bugger's buggering around wi' the pound. Aah'd bugger round wi' him if Aah could find out who it was.'

'But they can't just let the Brigade end like that; you said the sailors needed you.'

'Aye, fifty years ago. Afore the piers was built. Now they got these improved lifeboats an' rescue-helicopters . . .'

'But you're still the last resort. Storms get too bad for helicopters . . .'

'Oh, they'll look after us in a fashion, when the Watch House falls doon the cliff. Give us a sensible little hut to hold the rocket-trailer and Land Rover. But where's the fun in that? Nowhere to play billiards, or have our things around us. Then they'll have to *pay* fellers to man the rocket, and the *volunteer* spirit will be gone.'

'But the Watch House is irreplaceable. It'd make a super museum. You ought to publicize yourself – get grants from the Council. Get those fellows from Durham University to support you.'

Arthur looked mulish. 'We can't play billiards in a *museum*. The Durham fellers wouldn't hold wi' billiards.'

'All right. But you do need funds, don't you? You could put posters up . . . charge admission . . . write a guide-book and sell it.'

'Aye, we need funds. Can't even afford fifty quid for a coat of paint. Aah could get the paint cheap, too!'

'From a feller who's fond of a nice bit of fish?'

Arthur laughed, for the first time that afternoon. 'Aah like your Modern Thinking, Miss Anne. Aah'll have a word wi' Mr McGill, our secretary. He likes Modern Thinking too. You must meet him. Meanwhile, Aah better get on shoring up this cliff.'

Anne wandered on to the Middens, where they joined the cliff. The tide was coming in, but they were

65

still exposed. How ugly they were! So unlike her usual summer rocks on Scilly. The Manacles and the Rosevean were great fangs of rock, but at least they were clean, clustered with living barnacles and fresh with seaweed. The Middens were polluted and urban rocks, flat like a pavement, with the Garmouth sewers running across the top, grey dead mud and rusting tins in their nooks and crannies.

Flat rocks. She would need to be careful; the tide would come in quickly. But it was a foot below the rock-tops at the moment. She walked to the far tip, where the basket sat on its post. She found a rock higher and cleaner than the rest and sat down.

It was like being in a boat. There was water on three sides of her. She was right out in the middle of the Gar. The sun was drying up the rain, and the Watch House on its cliff looked far off, misty and dreamy.

An help pleas. What did the Old Feller want? She could bear to think about him, out here in the calm and the sun.

Then she laughed, because it was all so simple. She'd been a ninny not to see it before. He wanted help for his beloved Life Brigade, of course. If the Watch House fell down the cliff, he'd have nowhere to go. Nowhere to tease the old men who were his only companions. Nowhere to jog elbows, or make footsteps, or push things over in the silence. It was nice to realize there was such a thing as a harmless ghost.

Maybe she could help a bit. Try to write a guide-book; she liked doing history. It would give a bit of point to this pointless summer. It would pay Prudie and Arthur for her keep. It would show Mother she wasn't just a paper parcel to be dumped any old where.

She suddenly felt so happy that she stretched and lay back full-length. The steel post with its steel basket was right above her. Arthur said it was only a sea-mark: warning ships' captains, at high tide, of where the Middens lay. But probably during storms various bits of flotsam had forced themselves inside the basket, making it look like a cruel rusty cage; a prison. It was big enough to take a human body, crouched up.

How horrible to be fastened inside, as the tide rose! She sat up abruptly. And then she remembered the skull.

It had been toffee-brown.

What had Arthur said? The grey bones came from the Priory and the brown ones came from the Middens.

The skull had drowned by these very rocks. Perhaps its other bones . . .

She started up. Suddenly she wished the Watch House was not so misty and far away. But there was good old Arthur, waving and shouting. He was so far off, he sounded like a seagull.

She realized she'd been hearing that seagull through her thoughts for some time.

What did he want? He was pointing up-river.

Oh, a ship coming out of harbour; a tanker with a black funnel escorted by two tugs. From where she sat it loomed as high as a house. Super. As it rounded the last bend before the piers, the tugs yipped and cast off. Ropes falling like graceful snakes into the water. Then the tanker put on a surge of speed, as if hungry for the sea.

She watched it grow nearer and nearer. What *was* Arthur making so much fuss about? Probably he knew the captain personally . . .

And then she saw what Arthur saw. The bow-wave of the tanker, three foot high.

At low tide it wouldn't have mattered. The wave would have broken on the first ridge of the Middens and died.

But it wasn't low tide; the water had crept up as she dreamed, filling the nooks and crannies, leaving just the high tip of each rock showing. Reducing the Middens to a thin lace of black rock and reflected sky.

The bow-wave began eating the lace away like a man eating a sandwich. She turned and ran. But she could make no speed. The slime on the rocks, sun-dried before, was now like black oil with the seeping tide. Her feet skidded every step. She had to plunge into channels full of opaque brown water. Twice she fell, before the bow-wave swept past her.

It was neither strong nor deep. But every rock-top vanished, and she was left standing in a waste of moving water. Stand still, she said to herself. The wave will pass; the rocks will show again. Don't panic.

But bow-waves are never single. Wave followed wave and the rocks did not reappear. She threw herself towards the shore, blindly.

She hadn't gone three yards before she plunged into a hidden deep-cut channel. The waters closed over her head. She couldn't find the air, she couldn't find the light. She was lost in the dark, in an immense crowd of hard round slippery shapes. She tried to breathe and breathed liquid mud; she could feel the grains between her teeth. Down, down, tossed, battered, never to see light again. To become brown bone in the black mud . . .

Then a hand grabbed her and dragged her retching into the light. Arthur's face, suffused with rage.

'You little fool! What were you crawling like that for? You coulda drowned in two feet of water!'

She looked down. The water came no higher than her knees, and was completely calm again. The tanker was a distant blue shape between the piers. She was aware that some minutes had passed. 'Dunno,' she said. 'I just thought I was drowning.'

'But ye were never near drooning. Look, Aah pulled ye out wi'out getting watter over me wellies.' True enough, Arthur was as dry as a bone, except the right sleeve of his jersey. They waded ashore.

'Arthur, where's Van Diemen's Land?'

'Old sailor's name for Tasmania. Off Australia. Why?'

'It was a funny thought I had, when I thought I was drowning: *The captain was swept overboard, and the mate committed suicide, and the Hop Light was found drifting off the coast of Van Diemen's Land*. It sort of ran through my head. Why should I think a thing like that?'

'Aah have never,' said Arthur, 'prided meself on knaaing the minds of female women. That's why Aah never married. Meanwhiles,' he added, with a glance at the clifftop, 'God knaas what Prudie'll say. We'll have to get the doctor to ye.'

'But I'm all right now.'

'Ye've swallowed watter from that river. God knows what's in it. Aah've known people be kept in hospital three days for observation after swallowing that watter. And need a lot of injections. C'mon, keep moving, or ye'll catch your death an' all.'

8

'Doctor says you can get up this afternoon,' said Prudie.

Anne looked up from her twentieth love-story. She'd just finished off the beautiful personal assistant to a world-famous interior decorator. By holding her head-down in her own wallpaper paste. Very satisfying.

'Lovely! Thanks, Prudie.'

But Prudie seemed disposed to linger, tidying the already tidy room, picking up neatly folded clothes and refolding them. Prudie had something on her mind. Anne knew the only way to get it out was to plunge her own head back into her book.

'I'll have to write to your mother, Miss Anne.'

'Oh, *why*, Prudie?'

'You're too much for me, Miss Anne. Fainting and smashing show-cases and nearly getting drowned. I'm not so young as I used to be. I just can't take the responsibility . . . you coulda been killed, and then what would I have said to Miss Fiona?'

'But I *wasn't* drowned. I couldn't have drowned. The water wasn't that deep. I promise to behave. If I stay close to Arthur . . .'

'He's getting no younger either. It really upset him, you getting caught on the Middens like that. He's still not over it.'

Since Arthur had just walked past the window, whistling cheerfully as a cricket, this was really a bit thick even for Prudie. But she'd always had that trick of dressing other people up in her own emotions. In any case, this wasn't the time to argue.

'Oh, Prudie, I've *tried* not to be a nuisance.'

Prudie wouldn't look at her. 'I'm not *blaming* you, Miss Anne. We just seem to have had a lot of bad luck since you came.'

There was a thoughtful silence. Prudie had an infinite belief in good and bad luck. If she spilt salt, she really did throw some over her shoulder. Seeing one magpie had ruined many an outing. A dropped spoon meant a letter coming. If a picture fell off a wall, someone close was going to die. Sometimes people tried laughing her out of it; they never laughed twice.

'There's nothing for you to *do* round here, Miss Anne. It's no life with us two old fogies. Like calls to like. You need young friends and there's none round here.'

Anne thought frantically. Anything was better than London. And Mother nagging the whole length of the motorway and for ever after. And that creepy Uncle Monty who insisted on kissing you and kissed wet.

'I *have* met some people ... the keeper at the Priory ... Father Fletcher.'

'Oh, you've met Father Fletcher?' Although she was a confirmed chapelgoer, Prudie's face lit up. 'He's done ever so much good. The pensioners' luncheon-club and the youth club.'

'He's asked me along to the youth club on Saturday night. They're having a disco.'

That shook Prudie. She said meditatively, 'It'll mean friends your own age; stop you mooning round that Watch House. That's not natural in a young girl.'

'It's a dull place,' said Anne, and sighed disenchantedly. Prudie gave her an old-fashioned look; Anne had nearly overplayed her hand. But in the end Prudie nodded.

'All right, we'll see. Make new friends and steer clear of that Watch House, and Aah mightn't have no need to write to Miss Fiona.'

'C'mon, pet,' said Prudie. 'Aah'll iron that for you. Won't take a minute. The iron's hot.'

Anne sighed. Wouldn't Prudie let her do *anything*? She'd thought hard what to wear at the youth club, and finally decided on plain Wranglers with a Wrangler top. She'd dallied with a Friends Of The Earth T-shirt, then an Elton John one; but had finally plumped for a plain blue. Nothing for little cats to get their tongues round; nothing for them to pick holes in. Course, they'd pick holes anyway. But not such painful ones.

'Nice to see you going out enjoying yourself,' said Prudie, holding up the T-shirt to the light. Then she returned it to the ironing-board and hammered out a totally invisible crease. 'That Father Fletcher does grand work. Proper gentleman; no fancy airs. Sits down by the fire here wi' a cup of tea, just like one o' the family. Even if we are Chapel. Aye, but he's thin. That Vicar's wife doesn't take care on him.' Prudie spoke yearningly. You could tell she just longed to get her hands on Father Fletcher and feed him up as fat as a pig.

'Have a lovely time, chick. Make the most of it while you're young.'

Anne cycled along Front Street, steeling herself to expect nothing and worse than nothing. Tonight would be an unmitigated disaster. But if she didn't find friends . . .

The church hall was dragsville. Its noticeboard carried a home-made poster for a film called *God of the Atom*. The atomic explosion looked like a wilting pink lettuce. It was two months out-of-date, and flanked by the usual starving Biafran and a list of ladies doing altar-flowers.

The ceiling was high; the rafters still carried last year's Christmas decorations. On the stage was a woodland backdrop for a pantomime: the wilting-lettuce maniac had struck again. Beneath, a record-player squawked breathlessly. Two boys stood watching it, as if wondering whether to administer euthanasia.

Five other boys kept going out in pairs, then coming back with even greater fuss. Perhaps they were going to the cloakroom to comb their hair on a rota-basis? In between, they kept trying to push each other over. They spent a lot of time eyeing Anne. They kept urging each other in her direction; but they weren't in any hurry.

Five girls sat in one corner, being catty about three girls in another. Till they spotted Anne. Their eyes went over Anne's clothing item by item, about twice as thoroughly as the KGB.

Two other girls were playing table-tennis with spastic limpness. Spending twice as much time looking for the ball as actually playing.

'Like a Coke, hinny?' A worried little woman looked out of a serving-hatch. Seven brands of cans were arrayed in ranks, like the British Army before Waterloo. The little woman spent ten minutes explaining the pros and cons of the seven drinks, as if she was in competition with *Which* magazine. At intervals she said desperately either:

'I don't know what's keeping Father Fletcher,' or,

'We've got a disco tonight, but it's late. Perhaps the trains have broken down.'

It helped pass the time; but a third account of why the trains broke down finally drove Anne into the body of the hall. She sat down ten yards from anybody. The five in the corner watched intently as she opened her can of Coke. When it spurted, a tall dark girl whom the rest called Linda said, 'Oooooooooh!' and the other four fell about laughing.

Then Linda said, 'Oooooh!' loudly again, when Anne snapped her handbag shut. Anne was just wondering whether to walk out or claw Linda's eyes out when three tremendous handclaps came from the door.

It was Father Fletcher, suddenly overawed by the silence he had created.

'Erm . . . we're expecting a disco tonight. Except it's erm . . . late. Perhaps the trains have broken down . . .'

'Hoo bloody ray,' muttered someone from the back of the hall.

'Yes, erm, well,' said Father Fletcher, desperately

gazing round for further inspiration. 'Yes, and here we have ... erm ... Anne ... Anne ... who's come to join us this evening for the first time. She's spending the summer in Garmouth and I think she's feeling a bit lonely and out of things, so I told her we'd give her our typical warm welcome.' He walked over, took Anne by the arm and gazed round appealingly.

'D'you think he fancies her?' muttered Linda.

'Who'd fancy *her*?' chorused the Famous Four.

But Father Fletcher seemed deaf as well as blind. He went on hanging onto Anne till she blushed with embarrassment. It looked like the biggest disaster since David Cassidy got married, until the swing-doors of the hall swung open.

A figure in a white coat and mask like a surgeon pushed in a hospital trolley. There was a body lying on it, with a sheet over its face, as they do with dead people. An awful silence fell. Anne could only think there'd been some terrible accident. A car-crash they hadn't heard ... they used church halls sometimes ...

The surgeon pushed his trolley rapidly down the hall, looking neither right nor left. He had bony wrists, with black hairs growing on them. One bony wrist reached out and unplugged the record-player, which died with a squawk like a strangled chicken. The surgeon reached under the sheet that covered the dead body and produced his own electric plug. He plugged it in.

Anne thought wildly of heart-and-lung machines; of Frankenstein. This just wasn't happening. The surgeon turned, tall, glasses over surgical mask. He pressed a switch. A noise came from under the sheet.

'It's ... Doctor Death's Disco!' boomed a voice.

Then lapsed into Elton John's *Funeral for a Friend*. The surgeon whipped off the sheet to expose a stuffed dummy; then threw off the dummy to reveal a perfectly ordinary disco-deck. He pulled off his mask to reveal a dark monkey-face with hair hanging below his shoulders.

Father Fletcher recovered himself and clapped three times, obviously hoping to make a speech of welcome. But his hands came together without a sound, and his mouth opened and shut as silently as a fish's. Two massive amplifiers, slung beneath the trolley, brooked no argument.

Suddenly everyone was dancing and the hall was full. Anne was whirled away by a little ginger lad. She caught glimpses of Doctor Death wandering among the dancers, squirting them with water from a three-foot hypodermic syringe marked *Happiness*. When the racket finally stopped, she smiled at Ginger and went back to where she'd left her bag.

There was a girl sitting in the next seat now who grinned and said, 'I'm Fat Pat'. Anne smiled back. Pat was that kind of girl. Whether she was fat . . . she certainly wasn't skinny. Her thighs and bosom were generous. But she didn't bulge over her bra-strap or anywhere else. She had smooth tanned skin and blonde hair so long she could sit on it. Nice as a pint of milk. And she had a certain air of being above it all that could only mean one thing.

'Are you with Doctor Death?'

Pat chuckled. 'I'm *with* him. Not his girlfriend. He's off sex. Says it's the capitalist rat-race transferred to an inappropriate sphere.'

'Oh!'

'I'm the one he *talks* to. He has this big need to talk at present. He has this big need to talk all the time. But especially at present. He's busy changing his image. Says the audiences have taken over his present image and turned it into a psychic straight-jacket. I'm only scared he'll go all Ecology – I *hate* cow-manure.'

At that moment, the disco-deck emitted a series of bright blue flashes. The smell of electrical trouble filled the air, bitter and sharp. Doctor Death leaned over the deck from front to back, poking with a huge screw-driver. The blue flashes were replaced by strings of orange sparks. All the girls screamed except Fat Pat, who said, 'It's part of the act,' and went on talking.

A red volcano spouted up. All the girls screamed again, between joy and terror.

'If that lot don't watch it,' said Pat, 'they'll need to go and change their knickers.'

'But . . .'

'You get used to it,' said Pat. 'After a while you hardly notice.'

But Father Fletcher had noticed. He unplugged the disco with a furious gesture. Doctor Death simply flicked a switch and the unplugged disco went on playing, while Father Fletcher stood incredulous with the plug in his hand.

'Twelve-volt car batteries under the trolley,' said Pat. 'That always grabs the oldies, that bit. He got tired of oldies always pulling the plug on him. Actually, I wish he'd stop needling Fletcher. Fletcher's OK for an oldie.'

78

The good Father exercised his charity and the dance continued. Then Pat said:

'Oh, God, there goes one of those silly little cows now. Will they *never* learn?'

Linda was inviting Doctor Death to dance, twirling her hips in a more than clear message. She was a nice shape, and could really move it, black hair flying. Anne began to worry for her new friend.

'Don't fret for me,' said Pat. 'Worry about *her.*'

Doctor Death squirted Linda with his syringe, clinically, head on one side. Linda took this for some kind of encouragement and tried the harder. Then Doctor Death began to dance with her. He wasn't bad, considering the length of his arms and legs. The other dancers fell back in awe, moving their limbs in token shuffle.

Then the quality of the Doctor's dancing subtly changed. He began dancing like a girl; a sexy girl.

Anne gasped. He was doing a perfect imitation of Linda, only more and more exaggerated. Someone giggled, then everyone was laughing. In the end even Linda got the message, because people were falling about.

Linda stopped, pushing one black wing of hair behind her ear nervously, over and over again.

Doctor Death went on dancing, getting nearer and nearer to her. Suddenly she shouted:

'Poof! Rotten stinking poof!' and stalked to the door, face as red as a beetroot. Doctor Death followed her all the way, swivelling his hips. Anne thought the place was going to blow apart.

'She asked for that,' said Pat sadly. 'She's at the sixth-form college. She knows the way he feels.'

'Oh, it was cruel . . . cruel,' gasped Anne, wiping her eyes and quite unable to stop laughing.

'Yes, he is cruel,' said Pat. 'But only when people ask for it. She wasn't really interested in *him*. She only wanted him to drive her home, so she could have told her friends tomorrow all kinds of lies about him. Swanking. Silly cow.'

Doctor Death was coming over to them.

'Don't be scared,' said Pat. 'Just be honest. He won't eat you.'

Doctor Death bent down from his great height. He had black bristly eyebrows that met across his nose. His spectacles were the tinted sort; it was hard to see anything of his eyes except the quick flash of intelligence.

'This is Anne,' said Pat. 'She's staying with the people at the Watch House. She might be coming to the college in September.'

Doctor Death gave a ridiculous bow, then sat, bony hands on bony knees, and asked a thousand questions about the Watch House. What was the range of the rockets? How did they allow for the speed of the wind? Did they use nylon ropes or hemp? Under what conditions did ships go aground? It felt like being engulfed inside a mental combine-harvester. Anne kept saying, 'I'll have to ask Arthur,' with monotonous regularity.

'Don't bother,' said Pat. '*He'll* ask Arthur. I hate to tell you this, but your Watch House looks like being his next craze. Ah, well, it's better than cow manure.'

Anne looked up, startled. Doctor Death was gone, dancing a waltz with an old-fashioned hat-stand purloined from the far corner of the hall.

Pat said, 'Don't worry – he likes you.'

'He makes me feel so *stupid*.'

'He doesn't mean to. He's got an overactive brain. The health visitor warned his mother when he was two weeks old. Poor woman. Still, he's kind to his parents. His father really is a doctor – hence all the second-hand surgical gear.'

'Is he at the college?'

'Just left. Going up to London University. Poor old London. Still, perhaps they'll keep his mind occupied. That's the *real* problem. He sort of *eats* subjects – gobbles them up and spits out the pips. Astronomy, chess, hypnotism, radio-controlled model aircraft.'

'Sounds exhausting.'

'It is. Specially as I have to listen while he works it all out. Us two can take it in shifts now – I won't feel so outnumbered.'

For better or worse, Anne knew she was in.

9

The next day was the rare sort when everything went right. There was a letter on Anne's breakfast-tray. She didn't need to read the address on the envelope flap, *Croydon Car Components. Racing and rallying specialities.* She could tell from the oily fingerprints all over it. Daddy put oily fingerprints over everything. He even tasted of oil when you kissed him.

She opened it with a painful little flutter of happiness.

Dear Anne,

Just a line to say I got your card. Sorry not to have written before, but I've been up to my neck in it as usual. Yes, I am sleeping at the works. Mrs Robinson is doing my laundry and having meals sent in. I don't know why she takes the bother. I pay her to run my office, but I expect she is the maternal type. God knows what her husband thinks.

Well, we're still in business. I've let the drawing-office men go, because they had other jobs to go to. So that means I'm back at the drawing-board. I'm really enjoying myself – I hadn't realized how much I'd missed it. Expense-account lunches were never my scene – I can't think when I'm all dressed up and half tight.

I've kept the machinists on. That's what the house-money was for. They seem to appreciate it. Two have had me home for a meal. That's the trouble with success – it cuts you off from the people you work with. Now we feel all together, sink or swim, and we're all working like hell.

Unemployment is awful round here. The young ones don't seem to worry so much, but the older men are scared – they think that if they once get unemployed they'll be on the scrapheap for life.

The German deal fell through; but Malcolm is still buzzing round the continent like a bumble-bee. I don't know how he stands it, keep having doors slammed in his face. But he remains ever-hopeful, and has his eye on some Swedish rally-driver who he thinks might sponsor us in Scandinavia. Never heard of the guy – his name is unpronounceable – Gunnar something – but Malcolm says he has big connections. But you know Malcolm – everybody has big connections.

It's amazing how you settle down, once you make your mind up to sink or bust.

Your loving
Dad.

P.S. I have had Toby brought down here. There is a spare garage and a bit of waste-land for him. Mrs Robinson has laid on hay and oats, but I don't think he eats much of them, as the lads have got very fond of him, and he does pretty well for sugar-lumps and apples and sandwiches. I'm afraid he's getting a bit fat – there's no one to ride him. Hope this is OK.

D.

Anne allowed herself five minutes' disgusting snivel, but had only had two when Prudie called, 'Someone to see you, Miss Anne.' She sounded conspiratorial, almost gleeful. Another female voice could be heard through the wooden wall. The voice and Prudie were going hammer and tongs with gossip. It sounded like feeding time at the zoo . . .

It was Pat. And Pat's mother actually ran the Garmouth Women's Happy Hour. And played the harmonium lovely. Prudie was busy stuffing Pat with tea and seedy-cake, and Pat was cheerfully letting her. The threat of a letter to Mother receded to infinity. Prudie said six times it was nice that Anne had Made Some Friends at Last. Pat winked behind Prudie's back, but the wink had no malice.

Then Arthur looked in to say there was a funny feller at the door. Prudie asked whether he was selling something and to send him away as they had no money to spend on rubbish. Arthur said he wasn't that kind of funny feller . . .

Anne looked out. It was Doctor Death, clad in metallic-blue trousers, a yellow anorak and a tweed hat, looking like a Martian on a fishing-trip. The threat of the letter to Mother instantly returned.

Didn't they know, enquired Pat with infinite tact, that this was Timothy Jones, the doctor's son?

Oh, that was different. Doctor Jones was a lovely man, who had done a lot of Good Work and was as Well Liked as Father Fletcher. In fact, Prudie had wheeled Master Timothy in his pram when he was two; on a day-trip to Ryton from the Chapel. But his hair had been shorter then. Had he forgotten the way to the barber's?

It might have gone ill even then, if Prudie hadn't noticed the trickle of water on the kitchen floor. Her ancient fridge had Gone Again, and she must speak with the Electric.

The moment her voice could be heard, addressing the Electric in a piercing shriek that almost made the phone superfluous, Timothy whipped the back off the fridge, and, producing screwdrivers and spanners from an infinity of hidden pockets, began strewing the kitchen table with fridge-components. Arthur sat watching him with a basilisk impartiality, only flinching silently as Prudie's voice reached a new crescendo in the hall.

Finally, as Prudie informed the Electric he was no gentleman, and banged the phone down, Timothy found a simple loose connection and began sliding the components together again.

Prudie halted in the doorway, her mouth gaping as wide as the Gar. Timothy, his long fingers moving like greased lightning, slid the last component into place . . .

A blessed hum filled the room.

'By gum,' said Prudie, in a dire voice. 'By gum . . . he's an Electric Genius!'

Anne sat with her face in her hands, weak with relief, as the letter to Mother finally vanished over the horizon. She opened her eyes to see Timothy also being plied with seedy-cake.

'He's got a crop for all corn that one,' said Prudie admiringly. 'Just like our Arthur. I'd rather keep him a week than a month!'

Thus started the era of Timmo the Electric Genius. Anne could have got quite jealous, if it hadn't been for the frequent enquiries as to whether the barber had gone bankrupt. Arthur mentioned the searchlight . . . As he and Timmo were heading for the door, Arthur turned back and said:

'Aah mentioned your idea for a guidebook to Mr McGill last night, Miss Anne. He wants to see you. Aah told you he liked Modern Thinking.'

It was indeed a day of wonders.

Mr McGill opened the parcel of newspaper as if it was the Crown Jewels, and sniffed delicately.

'Plaice. Lovely.' He buzzed for his secretary. 'Miss Bell, I want you to put this fish in the safe. It's the coolest place in the office, and I want it kept *fresh*. See to it – your job depends on it.'

Miss Bell, a highly decorative piece who thought a lot of herself and would have liked Mr McGill to share her opinion, wrinkled her nose, but not so much that it showed. She gave Anne the same look as she'd given the fish.

'The Chairman of the Council is due in five minutes, Mr McGill.'

'Charlie Martin? Let him wait. He's kept me waiting often enough. Now *he* wants something off *me*, let him sweat a bit.'

He gave Anne a conspiratorial grin. He was the oddest solicitor she had met. He wore a suit with a waistcoat, like all good solicitors; but it had a rather loud check. With his long villainous moustache and sideburns, he looked like a cross between a Mexican bandit and a successful bookmaker.

'I want you to do this guidebook,' he said to Anne. 'And get posters ready for the Castle railings. I'll square the Town Planning people about the posters. They owe me a favour.'

The phone rang. Mr McGill's face assumed a near-criminal aspect. His voice went very vulgar. 'Plead Guilty, Len, for God's sake. Tom Wilburn's the beak at Tuesday's court, and he's always softer if you plead Guilty. I'll take the line that you'd never have pinched the oil if you hadn't been worried about your missus's operation. His missus has just had the same operation ... If you plead Not Guilty, with what the rozzers have got on you, you'll get three months, I swear it ...'

Eventually, he hung up, and grimaced at Anne. 'Funny how they cling to their illusions of innocence. *Who's* innocent? I'm not innocent. You're not innocent. Are you going to tell me you never stole a thing in your life? Not one solitary thing? Of course you're not.'

The phone rang again.

'Good morning, Sir Leslie. I trust you are well? Looking forward to the Carnival? We are most grateful for the loan of your garden.' Mr McGill had composed his face in a look of Establishment dignity. His voice was as smooth as a newsreader's. 'Oh, yes, your geraniums. Yes, I was very sorry about your geraniums. I'll set one of our Boy Scouts to guard them this year. You have my personal assurance. And dogs will be banned. We've put it on the carnival tickets. Yes, I saw to it personally – I have the tickets here in front of me ...'

He hung up and grimaced at Anne again. 'Silly old bugger. Thinks geraniums are more important than saving sailors' lives.'

'Sailors' lives?'

Mr McGill leapt from his chair and paced round

the room. He filled the place with a kind of benevolent fury. If you could imagine a caged tiger managing a whole zoo from its cage you had Mr McGill. 'Yes, sailors' lives. The Carnival. Half the proceeds go to the Lifeboat, and half to the Life Brigade. The Rotary Club runs it every year, and we make a right killing. That's why I want you doing the guide-book to the Watch House. Ready for the Carnival, 20th August. Can you do it? Arthur has all the old records. 'Course you can do it – I can see you're bright.'

He sat down again. Miss Bell buzzed. The Chairman of the Council had arrived.

'Give him this month's *Country Life*. Give him a gin. Give him your solace and comfort, Miss Bell. But just keep him off my back for ten minutes. I'm *busy*.'

'Very well, Mr McGill.' Miss Bell sounded considerably miffed. Perhaps her hopes of Mr McGill were starting to fade.

'I wish she'd get herself a young man,' said Mr McGill. 'Do her a power of good. You got a young man? No, 'course you haven't – not in Garmouth anyway. You've just arrived. What a bloody stupid question for me to ask.'

He looked at her suddenly with a new look. It dawned on Anne that Arthur had talked to Mr McGill about more than plaice and guidebooks. She realized that Prudie and Arthur were still worried about her; and that they always went to Mr McGill with their worries.

'Want to tell me about it?' asked Mr McGill gently.

Anne tensed up. She wanted to talk about Mother and Daddy, and yet she didn't. It was like that time

88

with Father da Souza. Only Mr McGill . . . well, he was a bit of a crook in some ways, and it wasn't so hard telling him.

She told him. When Mr McGill listened he really did listen; for half an hour, alert as a cat beside a mouse-hole. While the Chairman of the Council had to console himself in the waiting-room, with *Country Life* or gin, or Miss Bell's favours.

Then Mr McGill began to talk. He led Anne through a rabbit-warren of legal consequences and options, to which she could only reply, 'Yes, I see,' or, 'Really?' or, 'I didn't know that.' It was all so surprising that at the end she felt her eyebrows were permanently stuck up in the middle of her forehead.

In the end, Mr McGill said, 'It depends what you really want. When *you* know what you really want, you'll get it. You can fiddle anything you want in this world, if you want it badly enough.'

Then he said, 'Oh God, Charlie Martin!' and Anne was hustled out amidst a shower of advice and blessings, before she could blink an eye.

It really had been a day of marvels. She must write to Daddy again.

10

'Here's your teas, Miss Anne, Miss Pat. Shall I take Master Timothy's up to him?'

'Let him come down, Prudie,' said Fat Pat.

They had dragged an old wooden table onto the Watch House lawn. The lawn, freshly-mown by Arthur, gave off its blissy summer smell; August at last. Anne put down her biro and Pat her felt-tip, and they both stretched luxuriously.

'That's my last notice,' said Pat. '*T. C. Clarkson's Tubular Cork Lifebuoy* – whatever *that* is, when it's at home.'

'It's hanging by the billiard-room door,' said Anne. 'You *have* done all the notices beautifully. And Timmo getting that perspex to cover them – it looks like a *real* museum now.'

'I'm glad some good's come from my misspent hours in the college art-room.'

'Except,' said Anne, setting her jaw, 'there's one notice you *can't* write.' She nodded at the great grey figurehead that was set in the ground across the lawn.

Pat groaned. 'Not again!'

'Well, I don't like being beaten. That's the one ship-wreck relic I haven't been able to trace. There must be a clue to it *somewhere*.'

'You know there isn't,' said Pat. 'You must have looked a hundred times.'

But Anne still picked up her teacup and drifted across to the figurehead. She ran a hand over the figure's decayed helmet and split shield. 'It's a soldier of some kind.'

'Yes, dear.'

'And you think it's Regency?'

'Between 1810 and 1850. At least that's what the figurehead book said. But that would be when it was made, not when it was sunk.'

Anne kept stroking the figurehead. She felt a slight depression, traitorous on such a lovely day. 'It's the best one and the biggest, and they leave it out here. They whitewash the rest beautifully, and just ignore this one. It's an antique worth thousands – and it's all split and rotting inside. Why do they leave it *here*?'

'You know why – because it's *always* been here. Like that eighteenth-century ship-painting on the staircase, hung in direct sunlight – cracked as Humpty-Dumpty. I told Arthur, and he's going to suggest it be moved at the next Annual General Meeting.'

'Meanwhile it goes on cracking.'

'I'd better get cracking and call Timmo.' Pat screamed up the Watch House stairs like a banshee. 'Timmo! Your tea's getting cold.'

'Down in a tick.'

'He never comes when he's called. He *likes* cold tea, with skin on top. He's *perverted*.'

Anne sat back, eyes closed, and thought what a difference a fortnight could make. She had friends. With the coming of Pat and Timmo, the Watch House had become no more than a happy workshop. Pat with her notices, Anne with her guidebook, and

Timmo working on the technical things with Arthur. The nicest thing was that Pat wasn't possessive about Timmo. After a fortnight, Anne could see why. Timmo was so erratic that Pat got quite lonely. Sitting at discos, night after night, while Timmo held the floor. Sitting at home two days at a time, when Timmo had a new bee in his bonnet and locked himself away in his workshop. And certainly, when Timmo was present, there was plenty of him to go round. He never stopped talking. But he didn't seem to mind who he was talking *to* providing they said, 'Yes,' occasionally, in a thoughtful way. Anne and Pat took it in turns to drift away as the flood of talk reached headache proportions.

Anne thought about the Old Feller, a little guiltily. He hadn't shown a sign for a fortnight. Perhaps because there was no longer any dust to write in; the Watch House shone like a new pin. The thought of the Old Feller still gave her a tiny cold thrill, but far away and fading in the warm sunlight. Had he ever really written in the dust? Anyway, she was doing what he'd asked. They were helping the Watch House.

There was a thunder of footsteps on the stairs.

'Hi!' said Timmo. He pointed to her sheets of paper. 'How's the magnum opus?'

'Nearly finished. I keep making neat copies, and Mr McGill keeps on scribbling all over them in red. He says lawyers can't stop scribbling on typescript – it's an occupational disease. Still, he'll have to stop it soon – Carnival's next weekend. He's going to have his secretary duplicate them.'

'How's the searchlight?' asked Pat.

'It'll live,' said Timmo. 'But jeepers – Arthur and his wiring. It's a wonder the whole place hasn't burnt down years ago.'

'Couldn't you . . .?'

'Don't look at me. I'm sick to death of wiring. And I'm sick to death of the disco. I need something new.'

'Just don't go back to hypnotism, that's all,' said Pat with feeling.

'What's wrong with hypnotism?'

'You play dirty tricks on the people you hypnotize.'

'You couldn't hypnotize anybody,' said Anne. 'Hypnotism's a fake, anyway – a music-hall act.'

Pat gave a faint groan. Timmo stared at Anne in his darkest, most unfathomable way. The silence lengthened. Anne realized that in some way she had gone too far.

Then Timmo whipped out his cigarette-lighter. It was typical of him that he carried a cigarette-lighter even though he didn't smoke. He flicked the lighter, and a long flame shot up like a sword.

Pat began laughing helplessly.

Timmo snapped off the lighter.

Pat stopped laughing.

Timmo lit the lighter again.

Pat fell about again.

Timmo snapped the lighter off.

Pat fell silent.

'Ask her what she's laughing about,' said Timmo.

'I don't know,' said Pat, in a baffled way. Then, 'Oh, you bastard, you rotten underhand bastard!' She attacked Timmo with some vigour. Timmo fended her off with one long arm, and snapped the lighter on again.

Pat collapsed laughing. Timmo turned to Anne with a look of dark triumph. 'I programmed her to laugh, while I had her under the influence. Every time I click my lighter. It's called post-hypnotic suggestion.'

'I told you he played dirty tricks,' said Pat, still helpless with mirth.

Timmo released her. 'C'mon, Pat. Let's show Anne how it works.'

'No more dirty tricks?'

'No more dirty tricks.'

'You won't let him play any more dirty tricks on me, will you, Anne?'

'No,' said Anne firmly.

'We'd better go inside the Watch House, then. If Prudie sees us, she'll have a fit.'

They trooped inside, and sat down in old armchairs. Pat seemed jumpy, but at the same time pleasantly excited.

'She'll go under easily,' said Timmo. 'I've done her so often.'

'Pooh,' said Pat. 'You'd think it was the hypnotist that did the work. Actually, it's the person hypnotized that does the work. Not everyone feels secure enough to let themselves go, but I'm good at it.'

She relaxed in the chair, eyes half-shut. Timmo took an old watch and chain out of his pocket, and swung it where Pat had to strain her eyes upward to look at it. Pat's eyes began to close. Timmo told her several times that she was feeling sleepy, falling asleep. Pat's eyes closed.

'You are now deeply asleep,' said Timmo. 'You will not wake up until I clap my hands twice. Then you will forget everything that has happened, and wake up feeling well and relaxed. Now open your eyes.'

Pat opened her eyes, smiled and stared about.

'You haven't done anything,' said Anne. 'It's a joke. She's perfectly ordinary.'

'Ordinary?' asked Timmo. He turned to Pat. 'You will feel no pain in your left hand.' He took a pin from his lapel, and jabbed it into Pat's hand. Pat didn't even wince; but a spot of blood formed.

'That's a dirty trick,' said Anne.

'Do you believe now?' asked Timmo.

'Yes,' said Anne, more for Pat's sake than anything else. She kept on looking from the spot of blood to Pat's smiling face. Timmo didn't do much more. He stood Pat up, told her she was a railway-sleeper that could feel no pain, and instructed her to fall flat on her back. Pat fell. Timmo only caught her, with an effort, inches from the floor. Her head banged a bit, but she went on smiling. Then Timmo clapped his hands.

Pat woke, beaming, and then said, 'Ouch!' She sucked her left hand, and rubbed her head. 'I see you didn't manage to stop the dirty tricks,' she said to Anne, tartly.

'Just scientific demonstrations,' said Timmo.

'Har, har, har!' said Pat. 'Vivisected the family dog yet?'

'Fancy having a go, Anne?' said Timmo.

'No,' said Anne firmly.

'No dirty tricks!'

'I'll make sure of that,' said Pat. 'I *know* him better than you do. I know where to kick him, so it'll hurt.'

Anne dreaded the thought; but they were the only

friends she had, and the friendship was too young to risk. What was a pricked hand and a bump on the head?

The watch swung over her, just on the edge of sight.

'You're feeling sleepy,' said Timmo monotonously. 'Your eyelids are getting heavier and heavier. Too heavy to keep open. Just empty your mind. Relax . . . relax.' It seemed to be going on for ever, and she had the most awful crick in the back of her neck. On and on and on . . .

'You are now deeply asleep,' said Timmo. 'Open your eyes.'

Anne opened her eyes. Peaceful. She no longer felt responsible for herself. Timmo was responsible now. Everything seemed slower and more detailed and more vivid; like the walks with Daddy, when she'd been a little girl.

Timmo looking triumphant; amused but kind. Pat leaning forward, was watchful, a little anxious about Timmo's intentions. Anne noticed for the first time the tiny incipient wrinkles under Pat's eyes; the fascinating curves of a few strands of hair that hung across Pat's ear. Between their two faces, a pale blue trawler moved slowly across a pale blue horizon . . .

Then the sun went out.

Darkness at every tall window. Oil-lamps swaying in the draught that swept the rocket-room. Men standing looking at her, from every corner. Pale faces, streaming oilskins. Outside, the wind battered furiously at the boards of the Watch House, carrying fistfuls of hail that whitened the windows and then vanished without trace. Timmo and Pat were nowhere. She wanted to scream and she couldn't.

Then one of the tall figures stepped towards her. The light from an oil-lamp made a shadow under his sou'wester. She couldn't see a face; just a chin with three days' growth of whiskers.

The figure stood obedient, expecting orders. Its mouth moved. It asked a question, but the Geordie accent was so thick she could only understand one word.

'Now?'

Something made her step to the window overlooking the Black Middens. The hail came, the hail cleared. And then she saw it, almost like a giant moth pressed against the glass. Dimly lit by a ragged trace of blue moon.

The sails of a great full-rigged ship, aground at the foot of the cliff. Some of the sails were just tattered streamers. As she watched, another split and tore to shreds before her eyes. Then another went, carrying a spar with it. It was like watching a daddy-long-legs beating itself to pieces against an electric lightbulb.

'Now!' shouted a voice behind her, and the men were moving. The thud of their boots on the floor-boards, the crackle of their oilskins as they shuffled forward in two long lines carrying ropes and posts and rockets. Someone opened the door, and then everyone was fighting the tearing force of the wind. Quite inevitably, she followed them outside. There was nothing she could do to stop herself. She had given up her will to Timmo.

On the clifftop, men leaning into the force of the wind. Three times the rocket-tripod was thrown

97

down. Finally it held, with two men clinging to each leg. She could see mouths open, sucking for breath like fish, as a rocket was lowered into place. Every so often a man would swim up through the gloom, asking for orders. So many trusting faces. Each time, though she was unable to make any answer, they went away satisfied. All the time they were shouting at each other, mouth to ear. But the wind and the waves drowned all.

A man took out something he'd been shielding under his coat; a lump of rope smouldering red at one end. He blew on it till it shone yellow, lighting up his whole face. He held it to a hole in the side of the tripod. There was a flash bright as lightning, and the rocket simply wasn't there. Only a dwindling spark, curving towards the doomed ship.

They had fired too far out to sea. But no, as the gale caught it, the rocket headed straight for the wreck almost buried in foam. Then the wind caught the rocket again, and it curved into the water on the land-ward side. A low groan came from the men.

Another flash, and another groan. Another flash and a cheer. The men round the tripod began paying out a heavier rope. Then a double-rope. Still they depended on her with trusting looks. Still she was unable to reply. Still they went away satisfied.

She looked round. The men on the rocket were no longer alone. Behind them, noiseless in the storm, a great half-circle of women had gathered, black shawls tightly round their heads. She could see their white faces turning this way and that, with every move, like a crowd at Wimbledon.

'Heave away, hinnies!' That came through clear

enough, and all the men by the rocket were digging their boot-heels into the turf like a tug-of-war team.

She looked towards the ship. The foremast was gone now, over the side. Its bulk lifted with every wave, and she heard the hollow *boom, boom, boom* as it struck the hull. But, much more important, a little bundle was working its way up the triple-rope; a little bundle with waving arms and legs. Helpless as a baby. Three times as she watched, the white waves buried it.

The third time, the bundle was smaller. It no longer had arms and legs. It was only a piece of canvas flapping in the wind.

There was an awful sound from the men and women.

'They've fastened the whip too low!'

'We sent them a clear notice. It was fastened tight to the whip-end.' A man held up a little black tin plate, pleadingly. It was crudely lettered in white: *Number 4. Make block fast well up mast. If no mast standing the highest place you can find*.

'They can't read English. They must be Froggies.'

'Russkies, more like, or a ship out of Latvia, by the cut of her jib.'

'What can we do now?' Every face in the crowd turned and looked at Anne. She could say nothing. But slowly she turned away to the cliff edge and looked down. Black rock; white foam. Black rock; white foam.

Men were screaming at her, pulling at her arms. 'Divven't try it, Henry! Ye'll never make it. It's barmy.' But she slipped off her oilskin. And coat and boots. The wind was like freezing arrows.

Then she wrapped her arms and legs round the triple-rope and launched herself off the edge of the cliff.

'Take up the slack, lads. Keep the rope taut, for Christ's sake!' It was the last sound she heard, except the waves. The ropes were slipping swiftly through her hands; water was squeezing out of them onto her face. The first wave reached up for her and there was only numbing blackness.

A pair of hands clapped loudly. Rafters above her head. A curving ship's nameplate saying *Iron Crown*. Then Pat's plump face looking down, creased with alarm.

'Pat!'

'Oh, thank God you're all right. I'll kill Timmo, I really will. I knew something like this would happen, one of these days. He ought to be certified.'

'I didn't *do* anything,' complained Timmo, close by her ear. 'Only the usual. I've done it *dozens* of times.'

'You've done it for the *last* time,' said Pat fiercely. 'The last time when I'm around, anyway.'

'Sorry, Anne,' said Timmo. 'I don't know what went wrong. I thought I had you under nicely. We were just arguing about sticking a pin in your arm when you jumped up and began shouting, "Who are they? Who are they?" Then you went running through the door, and nearly jumped straight over the cliff. We had to drag you back and hold you down.'

Anne suddenly realized that she was lying on the floor by the outside door, and both Pat and Timmo were lying heavily on top of her.

'Sorry,' said Timmo again. He got up and dusted himself off, looking embarrassed.

'I should *think* so,' said Pat, raising herself. Anne rubbed her stomach, where Pat's elbow must have been resting for some time.

The door swung open.

'Whatever's going on?' asked Prudie, crossly. 'All that running and wrestling and screaming. This isn't a children's playground, you know.'

'Sorry, Prudie. We were just having a doss with a bar of chocolate.' But for once even Timmo's charm didn't work.

'It's ten past five. Time you went home for your tea, Master Timothy. And time you had more sense. Aah won't tell Arthur ye've been messin' wi' his Watch House. It'd break his heart. You might have harmed something precious.' She picked up a *Guide to Seamanship* from the floor, as it if had been the Holy Bible.

Anne watched sadly as Timmo and Pat went dwindling up the road into Garmouth.

'Chocolate indeed!' said Prudie, and made for the door. But Anne pushed out in front of her, in a sudden panic not to be left alone in the Watch House.

'Manners, Miss Anne! Aah don't know what's got into you children today.'

11

'C'mon,' said Pat coaxingly. 'C'mon, you can tell *me*. I won't tell Timmo, honest. Not if you don't want me to.'

They were lying on the Watch House lawn the following afternoon. Timmo hadn't shown up; probably in a huff.

'Go *on*,' said Pat. She'd been saying it for half an hour, and looked like going on saying it for the rest of the afternoon.

Anne sighed; she didn't like this new side of Pat. This sort of feverish nosy hunger; this cosy creepiness. But she had a nasty feeling that if the feverish cosy nosiness wasn't satisfied, there'd be a row and Pat would go off in a huff too. And she'd lose them both. Timmo wouldn't come back if Pat wasn't there. When Pat wasn't around there was a stiffness between her and Timmo.

'All right, but it'll sound awfully silly.'

'Don't worry about *that*. After a year with Timmo, nothing would surprise me.'

Anne told her: the dark, the wind, the rocket, the terrible empty flapping canvas, the waiting ring of women, the waves . . .

'Is that *all*?' Pat sounded disappointed.

'What do you mean, *is that all*!'

'I thought you might have seen a ghost or something.'

'Well . . .?'

'Oh, c'mon, duckie. One ghost, maybe I'd believe that. But twenty ghosts, thirty ghosts . . . a ghost ship and a ghost storm and ghost oil-lamps? Sounds like a Hollywood epic by Cecil B. de Mille. Cast of thousands.'

'So what was it?'

Pat laid a hand on her arm. Why did people have this *touching* habit? 'A sort of dream, silly. I mean suppose you'd come to and instead of Timmo and me holding you down you'd found yourself in bed? I mean you've had these things on your mind for a fortnight non-stop now, doing your old guidebook. Shipwrecks, gallant rescues, rockets – I wonder they're not coming out of your ears. And I mean, well, you've been under a strain with your mam and dad . . . It's all right being hypnotized if you're a placid cow like me, but maybe hypnotism is like LSD trips – they can go sour if you're in bad nick when you start.'

There was a soothing note in Pat's voice that infuriated Anne.

'All right then. I'll tell you something that *really* happened.'

She told Pat about the writing in the dust. And the skull. Pat fingered the new putty Arthur had put in the glass case, then looked up, blue eyes shining and smooth cheeks very rosy.

'Oh, I like it, I like it. I can feel it now. I'm a sensitive, you know. My aunt told me I had gifts . . .

she's a spiritualist and she's taught me. Shall we try and make contact? I'm sure there's somebody there.'

Without waiting for Anne's answer she went scurrying round the billiard-room.

'Here's a smooth surface. Now, paper and pencil.' She tore a sheet of Anne's notebook into squares and began writing capital letters on them. 'We need a tumbler. Go and ask Prudie for a glass of water. Tell her I feel faint . . . no . . . that'll fetch her over fussing . . . tell her I feel thirsty.'

Anne went, but she didn't like it. She didn't mind lying to Prudie; but she disliked Pat *making* her lie to Prudie. When she got back, Pat had the bits of paper in a circle on the smooth polished surface. Pat drank the water in one gulp, dried the glass with a none-too-clean handkerchief, and set it upside down in the middle of the circle of letters.

'Sit down. Relax. Make your mind go blank. Put your first finger on the glass beside mine. No, don't press hard; just rest your finger lightly. There.'

Anne put her finger on the glass, but she didn't want to. She closed her eyes, but she still didn't want to. She absolutely refused to let her mind go blank. She'd let her mind go blank with Timmo yesterday, but this was silly childish rubbish. She despised people who played these games. So why was she shaking?

'We've had some marvellous results at my aunt's,' said Pat. 'She has a spirit-guide called Little Bear who was in America when the Pilgrim Fathers landed. He was a chief of a big tribe.'

A spurt of giggle almost burst its way through Anne's growing tension. Why was it always Indian chiefs? Who just happened to live at important historical moments? What happened to the spirits of unemployed Bermondsey dockers who died in 1922? Was it a case for the Race Relations Board?

'You're not *trying*,' said Pat plaintively. 'You've got to *believe*. They don't like it when there's an Unbeliever. I can *feel* you not believing. They won't come . . .'

Oh, for God's sake, thought Anne. Stop going on like a silly idle middle-aged woman.

'Is anybody *there*?' asked Pat, in a tone of melodramatic significance.

The tumbler remained quite stationary. Obviously nobody was.

'Is anybody *there*?'

Not a glassy wiggle.

'It's *your* fault,' hissed Pat. She sounded pretty cross. But Anne wasn't really listening; she had suddenly realized what was making her so uneasy. She was sitting with her back to the skull in the glass case. She had a growing urge to turn and look at it. She fought the urge down, telling herself it was silly, but the urge grew like a niggling itch . . .

'Is there anybody *there*?' demanded Pat again. She sounded angry, as though she would give Little Bear hell when she caught him. Anne sat paralysed, like an iron filing between two angry magnets; magnets getting angrier.

'Is there anybody *there*?'

The glass trembled; the glass vanished from between their fingers. There was a rending crash. Little sharp needles pricked Anne's face. She heard Pat cry out, and opened her eyes. There was blood on Pat's face: a thin trickle running down from her hair. The whole room was twinkling with points of light like frost: Pat's hair, the cover of the billiard table, the floor. Dazedly, Anne reached for a point of light. It was a fragment of glass like a needle.

'Look at that!' said Pat, awed. There was a scar in the sunblistered woodwork beside the window: a deep-gouged scar; half an inch deep. The window had escaped destruction by a fraction, and it was a huge expensive window. A window the Brigade could not afford to replace. It came to Anne that if that window had been broken, they would all have been banned from the Watch House for good.

'I moved my head and it hit me,' said Pat. A huge bump was showing through the edge of her hair. 'What was it? What was it?'

If Pat had not moved her head at the last second, and deflected the tumbler, it *would* have broken the window . . .

'Come and lie down next door,' said Anne. Pat came without a word. Anne made her lie down in one of the old armchairs, and staunched her wound. It did not bleed much, but the blue bump was developing into the biggest Anne had ever seen. 'Just lie still, while I go and clear up.'

She went back. She looked for the big heavy base of the glass tumbler, but she could not find it; it had gone into fragments like all the rest. She looked at the gouge in the window-frame. How much force . . . She shivered. She would have liked to run away and never come back. But she couldn't leave the glass, because she could never explain the glass. The whole room was covered. She picked it from windowsills, and from the light overhanging the billiard table.

Fragments glinted up on the picture-rail. But mainly it was on the floor. She crawled endlessly on her hands and knees, picking up the pieces. Pleading in her mind with the skull not to do something else. But never looking in the skull's direction. Crawled round on her knees like a servant, a scullery-maid, a menial, a prisoner.

The skull allowed her to finish. The skull allowed her to rub some dirt into the white gouge-mark on the window-frame, so it didn't show up to the casual glance. Then the skull allowed her to go. She felt a dull submissive gratitude to it; she wondered if she was going insane.

She went into the rocket-room. The sky had clouded over and the room was growing dark.

'Pat?' she said to the huddled figure in the armchair.

No answer.

'Pat?'

Pat stirred. 'Look,' she said. Anne looked where she pointed.

At the far end of the rocket-room, Arthur's model lighthouse was flicking off and on. It was between them and the door.

Side by side they watched the light, Pat lying in the chair and Anne kneeling beside her. Somehow they found each other's hands, and it was a bit of comfort. They stayed there a long time while the light flickered. Anne's legs got pins and needles and then went quite numb, but she didn't move.

She could tell Pat was a bit woozy from the bump on the head; not quite all there. For herself, picking up the glass had drained every ounce of will out of her.

It quietly got cloudier, darker. Nothing else happened but the flicker of the light. Anne was seized with a horrible cowering gratitude. After the awful violence of the tumbler, they were being let off lightly. It was as if Genghis Khan had summoned them, and then merely offered them tea and cakes.

If anything, the flicker was soothing; it had patterns in it. Some of the flashes were longer than others . . . almost like Morse Code . . .

Then the light stopped flickering; went out. They waited. Anne felt if it didn't come on again she'd *scream*.

There was the crash of a bucket being kicked over, and the outside door flew open. *Both* girls screamed.

'What the hell?' said Timmo. 'What are you sitting there in the dark for, like a pair of stuffed owls? You nearly scared the life out of me.' He banged on all the overhead lights by dragging his hand down the switches.

Both the girls stood up, blinking and feeling ridiculous.

'The light in the lighthouse was flickering,' said Anne feebly.

Timmo hauled the whole model up, exposing a tangle of twisted brown and yellow wires under the base.

'Arthur's bloody wiring – typical. Ah, here it is – wire loose from a terminal by a hair's breadth. I'll soon fix that.' He whipped out a screwdriver.

'No, don't,' said Anne.

'Why *not*?'

108

'Just don't – that's all.'

'Suit yourself. What's the matter with you two, anyway?'

They took him into the billiard-room, and showed him the scar on the window-frame.

'Jeepers – that's solid oak. How'd you do it? Sledge-hammer?'

'A glass tumbler.'

'You're kidding. Even Tarzan couldn't have done that with a glass tumbler. Where's the tumbler?'

Anne mutely held up the old cake-bag she had used to collect the pieces. Timmo picked out one piece and whistled. 'Some impact. Whoever threw it is the next Olympic champion.'

'It threw itself,' said Pat. Her voice was no longer scared, just defensive. Anne realized she, too, was no longer scared. She looked at the skull in the case and it was just a skull in a case.

'Oh, *no!*' said Timmo in disgust, picking up a square of paper with a capital N scrawled on it. 'Oh, no, Pat, not *that* stupid tumbler-writing act again. "Come in, Little Bear, we are receiving you loud and clear. Please land on Runway Nine." '

'Shut up!'

'Look, I spent two flaming weeks investigating tumbler-writing, and the tumbler never even moved. Till I turned my back. Then it began writing a hundred-thousand word novel.'

'It's your unbelief. You'd frighten *anything* away. You even frighten living human beings away.'

Anne looked at the skull in the case again, con-temptuously. It was true what Pat said. Timmo did frighten things away. She couldn't believe that silly

109

lump of bone had done anything. Not because the electric lights were on, but because the room was full of Timmo: cynical, searching Timmo, waiting to tear the guts out of anything that moved and hold it up for scientific inspection.

'Timmo,' she said. 'When was Morse Code invented? Was it very long ago?'

Timmo put four fingers to his forehead, as if he was turning on his memory like a radio-set.

'Longer ago than you'd think. Samuel Finley Breeze Morse invented his code for the telegraph in 1835. Soon after he'd invented the telegraph itself. American gent – artist, actually. First message he sent was "What hath God wrought?".' He paused and looked at her. 'That was a bloody funny question. What you up to?'

'I think . . . that model lighthouse was sending messages in Morse Code.'

'*Yewhat?*'

She said it again; nearly as scared of him as she had been of the skull.

'Oh God, you're as bad as Pat. Worse in fact. You're a perfect pair. How can women expect equality with men when they go on this way?' The contempt in his voice hurt.

'You haven't explained that tumbler yet, Sunny Jim,' said Pat viciously. 'How'd you explain the tumbler and that scar in the wood?'

'Poltergeist activity, eh? Just like Borley Rectory? Well, let me tell you something. All your so-called experts say that poltergeist activity – *alleged* poltergeist activity – is associated with unbalanced adolescents – usually female.' But there was curiosity

110

in his voice now, mixed up with the contempt. He looked at the splinters of glass again. 'You wouldn't have another tumbler, would you? Another tumbler I could throw for comparison?'

'No,' said Anne firmly.

Timmo sighed. 'Well, you better come next door and sit down and tell your Uncle Timothy the whole thing from the start . . .'

12

Sleep, daylight and breakfast destroy terror, wash it away as a morning tide cleans a beach. Even the figureheads with their white eyes looked benign in the sunlight flooding the rocket-room. Anne sat in one of the Watch House armchairs, a scribbling pad on her knee, and waited in vain for something to happen.

'I must have disturbed that wire last night,' said Timmo, after twenty minutes. 'You see, when a wire's just touching a terminal, the current passing through warms the wire, so that it expands and bends away, and the contact's lost. Then the wire cools, and comes back to the terminal. So you get a flicker.'

'It's not that,' said Pat, still sulky from last night. 'It's *you*. It won't do anything while *you're* around.'

'OK,' said Timmo. 'Bye bye!' He got up, put his hands in his pockets and strolled to the door.

'Hey – don't go too far away,' said Pat nervously.

'Why not?'

'We'll need you to read the Morse Code.'

'Pah!' He went out, passed the windows, and made for where Arthur was mowing the grass of the clifftop. Two heads immediately bent over the sputtering lawn-mower.

'Look,' said Pat triumphantly. 'There. Quick, take it down.'

The lighthouse was flickering. Anne's stomach

112

turned over, but she scribbled down the dots and dashes as Pat read them out. Pat's voice was quick and breathy. After about ten minutes the flickering stopped. Anne looked at her notebook.

. . . . . — — — . . . . — — — . .

'I can't read *that*,' said Timmo, hastily summoned. 'You idiots! You haven't left any gaps – didn't you notice any longer pauses between letters? I can't tell where one letter stops and another starts. This could read SUZSUZ or ESAMIE or IEUMS or *anything*. Maybe the Old Feller wants you to suzsuz your ieums, and about time too, I say. But otherwise—'

'Get out,' said Pat, very narked. 'You might have told us.'

They settled down to wait again. But the light had just started to flicker when Prudie walked in with coffees. They saw with sinking hearts that she was in a talkative mood; fussing; all ready to twit Timmo about his hair when he came back to see what was going on.

When she finally went, Timmo looked at his watch. 'How much longer is this going to take? I've got things to do.' He sounded bored, but hung around till lunchtime. The lighthouse remained obstinately dark whether he was in the room or not. He wrote out the Morse Code for Anne before he went; that meant he wouldn't be coming back. Not for quite a bit. Anne could tell from his restless moving about. He was bored with the Watch House; something new was stirring in his ever-fertile brain.

Pat was vague about coming after lunch, too. She was in a clingy mood, wanting to follow Timmo about; scared of losing a place in any new enterprise.

113

By three o'clock, neither of them had shown up. Anne felt very miserable; somehow it was lonelier than before she'd met them. Maybe they'd just drift away and she'd be back at square one . . .

Unless the flickering light paid dividends. She squared her shoulders, and marched back to the Watch House, scribbling-pad in one hand and pencil in the other.

She pushed the armchair up closer to the model lighthouse, and away from the door to the billiard-room. She went back, and closed the billiard-room door quickly, without looking inside. She looked out of the window. The headland seemed completely deserted. Arthur had a transport job down at the Quay, and Prudie had gone shopping up Front Street. There was a man walking his dog further down the cliff, but he soon vanished from sight. She did wish he hadn't.

But what was there to be scared of? This was the same room she'd sat in this morning, drinking coffee with Prudie and Pat and Timmo; joking and laughing. What was the matter with her? Why couldn't she be tough-minded like Timmo?

She began thinking about the skull. She wished she wouldn't start thinking about the skull. It was when she started thinking about the skull that things happened . . .

The skull became clearer and clearer in her mind. Every horrible stain and crack in it. She tried blotting it out with Daddy's face, but she couldn't remember Daddy's face half so clearly . . .

The lighthouse started to flicker. She whimpered to herself, but began to copy down the dots and dashes and gaps. If she was a good girl, and did what the Old Feller wanted, he wouldn't throw anything. He'd only thrown the tumbler to drive them out to the model lighthouse. He hadn't hurt them . . . well, Pat's head, but not much. He was a canny little feller . . . Arthur had said so. Everyone had liked him.

But it wasn't *his* skull.

The lighthouse stopped flickering. She bolted out into the sunshine of the cliff and sat down till she'd stopped shaking. Then she began to translate the dots and dashes:

AN HELP AN HELP WARE HAGUE WARE HAGUE HAGUE HAGUE HAGUE HELP.

It was the Old Feller all right. And the word *Ware* and the word *Hague*. There was a town called The Hague. In Holland. There was a town called Ware in England. There was a joke about it. The great Bed of Ware. But what had either of them to do with the Life Brigade or the Watch House?

'Well,' said a familiar voice behind her. It made her jump a foot in the air. 'Well, look who we've got here. The Madonna of the Tombstones. Only *we're* eavesdropping on *her* this time. What have you got there, sweetheart?'

It was Father Fletcher and Father da Souza, coats over their arms again. They dropped down one on either side of her, and stared intently at the scribbling-pad.

'I'm learning Morse Code,' said Anne feebly. 'Trying to teach myself.'

Father da Souza picked up the pad. 'An. Help. Hague. Ware. A bit monotonous.'

115

'Oh, I was just fooling. Playing games with myself.'

But Father da Souza wasn't as easily put off as most adults, who only asked you questions out of politeness. Father da Souza really wanted to know.

'Why was your writing shaking so much?'

'I was trying to write without looking at what I was writing.'

'That would make writing sprawly but not *shaky*.'

'I was with some friends. They were making me laugh. Just fooling about.'

'Hmmm.' He wasn't convinced. He went on staring at the notebook.

'Oh, stop trying to psychoanalyze people all the time,' said Father Fletcher crossly. 'I wonder you have any friends at all.'

'Right,' said Father da Souza. He closed the notepad with a snap and gave it back to her; tried to catch her eyes, but she wouldn't look at him.

'How'd you enjoy the youth club the other night?' asked Father Fletcher. 'Disco wasn't bad, was it?' Dear blind Father Fletcher. He wasn't even listening to her answer.

'We have come,' said Father da Souza, 'to inspect your Watch House.'

Anne gave a guilty jump. Father da Souza noticed.

'Will you take us round and explain things to us?' he said quietly. 'You promised you would. We've been looking forward to it.'

The Watch House door was swinging in the wind; she'd run out and left it. Notices were flapping wildly on the notice-board, and some litter had blown in.

'Hallo,' said Father da Souza. 'It's open already.

Who's in charge?' He poked his head in and shouted 'Hallo?' loudly.

'I'm in charge,' said Anne.

'Is it a good idea just to leave the door open like this? Aren't there valuable things . . .?'

'Yes. It was silly of me. Sorry. I forgot to close it.'

'Oh, leave the poor child alone,' said Father Fletcher. 'Shoot us the works, Anne!'

She led them up and down the rocket-room. Explained the model of the breeches-buoy. Father Fletcher turned the handle enthusiastically, and Action Man tapped his heels.

'Catch me in one of those things!' said Father Fletcher. But he liked the model ships, especially the ones with rows of brass portholes. Rambled on about watching model steamboats on a park lake when he was a little boy as if he was an old man of ninety, instead of twenty-five.

Father da Souza said nothing. Just stared at the souvenirs from the wrecked ships which hung from the rafters. He'd put his coat back on, and for some reason the coat-collar was turned up. The more he was silent, the more Father Fletcher babbled.

Suddenly, Father da Souza shivered.

'What's the *matter* with you?' asked Father Fletcher abruptly. 'Sickening for flu or something?'

'This place depresses me.'

'Why? It's a bit of a junk-shop, but it's fascinating. All these old things . . .'

'Yes, all these old things. Why do people pile them here?'

'To remember, I suppose. Like in churches.'

'Like in the Church of *England*. Regimental flags.

117

Rolls of Our Glorious Dead. Old medieval helmets. What's that got to do with Christianity? The Church of England is the Museum of England.'

'Oh, come. The Church of Rome is hardly backward with relics.'

'Oh, yes, we have relics. Relics of holy men and women. Who died confessed and shriven. Who gave up their being to God, *consenting*.'

'Stamped with the approval of Mother Church, like the Egg Marketing Board used to stamp eggs?'

Anne stared aghast, from one curate to the other. Why were they squabbling? They'd been good enough friends when they met her on the cliff.

'We of Rome believe that holy relics may have some helping power. People may laugh at us, but at least we're sure that if our relics do no good, they certainly do no *harm*.'

'What do you mean?'

Father da Souza pointed to a mummified seaman's cap, that hung brown on a nail. Its cap-band said *HMS Iron Crown*.

'What happened to the man who owned that cap?'

'The *Iron Crown* was sunk,' said Anne. 'In a storm.'

'Exactly. His cap was snatched from him by a storm. His life was snatched from him by the same storm. Robbery with violence. How did that man feel in his last moment? Frightened? Despairing? Enraged at his Creator, who was cheating him of life? If holy relics have good vibes, what kind of vibes would you expect this to have?'

'Perhaps he survived,' said Father Fletcher.

118

'Then why didn't he come back for his cap? It's marked with his name.'

'Oh, come . . .'

'Oh come, oh come . . . I am sick to death of your Anglican oh-comers. Whenever any question gets too uncomfortable, you get out of it by saying "oh come". Would you have this cap in *your* house, hung by *your* bed?'

'No.'

'Yet here all these things are clustered together. Can't you feel . . .' He broke off, and looked out of the window at the river. Then he turned again, and gestured at the rafters.

'Does *your* church take responsibility for these dead?'

'I presume they received Christian burial.'

'You presume too much. Do all drowned bodies come to land for Christian burial?'

'No,' said Anne, closing her eyes.

'No,' said Father da Souza, staring at the river again. 'Many must lie there still unburied, under the mud and sewage and Coca-Cola cans.'

'Surely a merciful Providence . . .'

'That's the trouble with you of the Church of England. You see Heaven as a kind of Welfare State, with everyone entitled to benefits. We of Rome are not so wholesale. We say *if* a man makes a good deathbed confession; *if* he receives absolution and the Last Rites, his soul goes safe to Purgatory. Do you think we give the Last Rites as a joke? Without them, we make no promises.'

He walked up and down the rocket-room restlessly. 'Is this all there is?'

'Yes,' said Anne.

'What is in here?'

'Only the billiard-room. Where the old men play billiards.'

Father da Souza opened the door and went in.

'Take no notice,' said Father Fletcher. 'He has these moods. It must be rough being a Catholic *and* an American.'

Father da Souza came out of the billiard-room. He looked paler and more hunched-up than ever. 'Only where the old men play billiards,' he said, and looked at Anne.

There was a long silence.

'Come on, old broody,' said Father Fletcher. 'Come up to the Garmouth Arms and I'll buy you a jar.'

'I do not want a jar,' said Father da Souza. He walked up very close to Anne. 'I don't know what you are up to, young lady. And it's fairly clear you're going to refuse, on the grounds of Protestant Free Will, to tell me. You will say it is none of my interfering Church's business. Given half a chance, no doubt you will quote the Inquisition at me. But,' he drew a handkerchief out of his pocket and wiped his fingers, 'whatever you *are* doing, I would urge you to stop, *now. Now.*'

He walked away to the entrance, where a highly-polished brass plate said: *Visitors desirous of contributing to the Funds of the Brigade are requested to place their donations in this box.*

He dropped four coins through a slot. They made a hollow noise.

Somehow, the way he dropped in the coins made

the whole Watch House seem like a church. A church where *what* was worshipped?

'Goodbye. If you ever feel like talking to me, here is my telephone-number.' He put a small square of white card in Anne's hand, and was gone.

'Don't fret about it,' said Father Fletcher. 'He's just trying to poach my flock, with a bit of fire and brimstone thrown in. An old Catholic trick. See you at the youth club.'

And he hurried off to join his friend.

Anne stood a long time watching the two black figures ascend into Garmouth and vanish; stood with the keys to the Watch House in her hand. She would have liked to have locked the door and never gone back.

But it was three days to the Carnival. Things were expected of her. She had no idea how she was going to get through.

13

Next morning, Anne was wakened by fog-horns. The North Pier, sounding brash. The South Pier, sounding plaintive. Two lonely giants, shouting into nothingness. The only thing visible in the world was the faint outline of the Watch House.

Breakfast was jumpy. Prudie kept wondering if she had enough tea and coffee, even though both her canisters were full. And what about milk if the milkman couldn't get through? Them old fellers never stopped drinking tea, once they got busy. Anne presumed the old fellers were the Life Brigade in action.

Arthur kept wiping the moisture off the window with his jumper-cuff, and peering in the direction of the Black Middens.

'Settle yerself, for Heaven's sake,' snapped Prudie. 'Aah've just washed that jumper an' ye'll leave greasy marks all over the window. Ye'd think ye *wanted* there to be a wreck.'

Anne decided against the Watch House that morning. It was spooky enough out-of-doors. But she soon got bored. She decided to seduce the Gallower; she still had three wizened apples from the bag she'd bought on her first day in Garmouth. She put on her coat and scarf.

'And where are you going, miss?'

'For a walk.'

'Tisn't fit for man nor beast,' said Prudie. 'Ye'll catch your death.' But it was a general sort of remark; she wasn't making an issue of it.

'Don't go near the cliff,' said Arthur, 'or ye might start parachute-jumpin' wi'out a parachute.'

The Gallower grazed the cliff-top freely, never strayed; Arthur said it wasn't faithfulness, just idleness and cupboard-love. She found him without much bother, staring at nothing in particular, his coat dark and heavy with moisture. Impossible to feel he was lonely or miserable or even bored. He didn't bother to look at her, until she rustled the paper-bag. He knew what paper-bags meant; he laid his ears back nastily.

She offered an apple; correctly of course, palm absolutely flat, apple balanced on top. It always made her nervous, with a strange pony: letting the soft lower lip quest round the tips of your fingers, knowing formidable teeth were only an inch behind. In this case teeth that had bitten through the wing of a motorcar.

His lip came in *much* too low; right under her fingers. She snatched back her hand just in time, felt the yellow teeth graze her fingernails. The apple fell to the ground. The Gallower sniffed and ignored it, and looked back expectantly at Anne.

She picked up the apple and tried three times more. Then, looking at the sly little eyes watching her, she came to a reluctant conclusion. The Gallower didn't like chewing apples; he preferred chewing people.

Defeat made her miserable. She'd always been proud of her touch with animals. She was losing her grip. She stared into the pale grey blankness around her; it was a day for losing your grip.

No, she was *damned* if she was going to lose her grip. She would get a grip on *something* and then she'd feel better. But not Pat . . . or Timmo. They were too important and she knew she was feeling a bit wild; in the mood where she made daft mistakes. No, that dog, that Priory dog. If she made a mess of *that* it wouldn't matter.

The top of the Priory Gatehouse was out of sight, up in the mist. She plunged into the dark tunnel, floored by wet cobbles. The curator slid back his glass window an inch, said she could go in free, broke out in a fit of coughing and pulled his nose back inside quick. It was not a day for reciting *The Burial of Sir John Moore*.

Avenues of tombstones faded away right and left. The grass soaked her shoes. She wished she'd brought wellingtons. Where to look? Why, in fact, was she so sure the dog would be here?

Just start, girl.

She came on signs almost immediately. The grass of one grave had a deep hole in it. Scored with pawmarks. The loose soil was fresh, not smoothed by the damp. The grave had been attacked before. New turfs had been laid here and there, in a kind of patchwork. Some had taken root, some withered. A battleground between dog and curator. She read the inscription on the tombstone.

IN LOVING MEMORY OF
JOSEPH BEAVERS, FOYBOATMAN
DROWNED SAVING LIFE

124

14TH OCTOBER 1854, AGED 27.

Anne looked next door.

WILLIAM MANLEY, MASTER-MASON,
AGED 87.

The turf of that grave was untouched. She checked the next twenty graves. All the dead lay unmolested. But the twenty-first grave had been attacked again and again.

ROBERT JOHNSON, RIVER-PILOT
DROWNED. FEBRUARY 2ND 1855. AGED 24.

After that, it became an obsession. She crossed and recrossed the clammy ground, looking for the tell-tale, tattered turf. She found a stub of pencil in her pocket, and wrote down the inscriptions on the defiled stones. Five graves. Five, out of hundreds. It didn't make sense. She read through the list. She noticed four similarities between those buried in the graves the dog had attacked. After that, she couldn't get out of the graveyard fast enough.

But Front Street was as empty as the graveyard. A few lights glowed dimly from shops. Cars passed at walking-pace. But the Memorial Clock and Drinking Fountain, the lamp-posts and garish hoardings seemed as thin as the scenery of a play, with only the fog and the sea-sound for audience.

She fled north up the promenade. The wind was moving the fog now. Sometimes she could see fifty yards ahead, sometimes nothing. Once she saw a dim figure standing, on the edge of vision. She almost turned back. But it was only an old man waiting for a bus that might or mightn't come.

Fog drifted through the ornamental gates of Garmouth Park. Then she heard men's voices shout-

125

ing in the murk. Like fog-horns, only merrier. She crept in, to be near.

No one by the boating-lake; just a fading expanse of choppy water. No one on the fog-grey bowling-greens. The pavilion loomed; she was nearly at the far end of the park. The voices got louder; but where? This was *mad*!

Then she looked into the sunken tennis-courts. A stocky figure in shorts was just visible, holding a racket. As she watched, a dim ball plummeted from the sky, bounced, and vanished upwards again. But the figure, judging its flight, ran across neatly to the place where it reappeared. He caught it with his hand and paused, listening.

'Come on, you cheating bastard,' came an invisible voice from across the net. 'I can *hear*, you know!'

The stocky figure ran across the court to a totally different place, and belted the ball back, hard. There was the thump of the ball bouncing, then a crash as the invisible someone hit the side-netting. The stocky figure doubled up laughing.

'Forty-fifteen!'

A flood of abuse came across the net.

'That *was* cheating,' said Anne severely; then blushed at saying such a thing to a complete stranger.

The stocky figure turned. 'Of course it's cheating. He's cheating, too. We've got to do our sinning *some-where*.' It was Father da Souza, face sweating and a big D on his T-shirt.

'Oh,' said Anne.

'Oh,' said Father da Souza, equally taken aback. 'Have you come to see me?'

'No. Just having a walk.'

'Some morning for a walk.'

'Some morning for tennis.'

A ball came hurtling through the mist and hit Father da Souza in the small of the back.

'We invented this game ourselves,' he said, picking up the ball thoughtfully and slamming it back like a rocket. As an afterthought he shouted, 'Out! My point!'

'What are you doing?' roared the fogbound Father Fletcher.

'Talking to a lady.'

'You don't know any ladies. Only wretched fornicating unshriven *sinners*!'

'You know this lady, too!'

'You mean there's really somebody there?'

'The secretary of the Mothers' Union. With the Bishop's wife.'

'You're joking.'

'Come and see for yourself,' said da Souza smugly.

'Oh, God. I think I'll stay where I am.'

'Where's your Christian fortitude, Father?'

The game resumed. Anne leaned on the dripping wire-netting, watching.

'This is the wickedest, most-cheating, most-lying game in the world,' rejoiced Father da Souza. 'It gets us in training for the other six days of the week. Father Fletcher is doing his imitation of the Devil, going about as a roaring lion, seeking whom he may devour . . .'

'Whom resist steadfast in the Faith,' roared Fletcher, sending, by hearing alone, a shot straight at his colleague's face.

127

Father da Souza volleyed neatly, replying, 'But Thou, O Lord, have mercy upon us . . .'

'And grant us Thy Salvation.' Fletcher's return just clipped the backhand corner.

'Game!' shouted Anne.

'Thank you, unknown friend,' shouted Fletcher. 'An angel in disguise.'

'The Devil disguised as a Child of Light.'

But the fog was clearing now. Father Fletcher became ghostily visible across the net, clad in old-fashioned, long-trousered tennis whites, with a school-tie tied round his slim waist. The game relapsed to ordinary tennis; but tennis of no mean order. Da Souza bounced round the court like a rubber ball, all muscular arms and hairy legs, firing off a succession of cannonball drives. By comparison, Fletcher seemed almost languid: long arm reaching out into the furthest corners to return the cannonballs by the power of their own momentum.

Until finally, having tried three times to pass him at the net, Father da Souza hit him smack in the stomach with a storming backhand.

'Urrgh,' said Father Fletcher.

'Whom the Lord loveth, Father, he chasteneth,' said da Souza with a certain satisfaction.

'I surrender! If I fall, who will chair the Roof Restoration Committee tonight?'

Father da Souza cocked an eye at Anne. 'Will no one rid me of this troublesome priest? Care for a knock-up?'

Anne, who had begun to drift away, couldn't resist the challenge, and borrowed Father Fletcher's racket.

'May the Lord have mercy on your soul,' said

Fletcher. Anne soon saw what he meant. The stocky priest didn't moderate his forehand in the slightest. It was a danger to life and limb. She didn't even touch his first five shots. Then she took a page from Father Fletcher's book, just sticking her racket out rigidly and letting the drives bounce off it. If you blocked him two or three times, da Souza usually hammered his next shot into the net.

When at last they collapsed on to a bench in sweaty heaps, Anne felt three hundred per cent more cheerful. But she didn't miss the look that passed between the two priests.

Father Fletcher got up, murmuring vaguely about fetching Cokes from the sea-front café.

'You *were* looking for me,' said da Souza suddenly.

'No, I wasn't,' said Anne.

'But there *is* something on your mind?'

'Perhaps.'

'Don't you think you've messed about with it long enough?' It was just like the tennis. Sudden aggressive jabs from the priest; Anne stonewalling them. Only now they sat side by side, staring at the surface of the court. A first faint touch of sunlight yellowed the cracked tarmac.

'Why do you play here?' asked Anne. 'Why not join the tennis club?'

'And have the people at the bar fall silent the moment we join them? Having your opponent afraid to swear when he muffs a shot because he's playing a priest? Here we can be ourselves.'

It came to Anne there was more than one kind of loneliness.

'There. I've been open with you. You know now

we're not plaster-saints. Why won't you be open with me?'

'All right,' said Anne. But Father da Souza gave a sigh of satisfaction that was a little bit *too* self-satisfied . . .

'It's that dog in the Priory. I've been looking for it again. It's digging the graves up.'

'Oh, *that* dog,' said Father da Souza, manfully hiding his disappointment. 'Well, we knew all that already.'

'But it only attacks five of the graves, over and over again. Never touches the rest.'

'Softer soil?'

'And they're all graves of drowned men.'

'Garmouth Priory graveyard is full of drowned men.'

'Who all worked on the river – foyboatmen, pilots.'

'The river is where men get drowned.'

'They were all *young* men.'

'Men died young then.'

'And they were all drowned between October 1854 and July 1855.'

'And so were buried all together in one place?'

'No, they're spread out all over the churchyard.'

Father da Souza was silent a long time. Then he said, 'You may have a point there. Won't you continue?'

'Cokes up,' shouted Father Fletcher from the terrace above. You could tell he knew he'd come back too soon. Father da Souza shot him a look like a dagger.

'What were the drowned men's names?' said da

Souza desperately, as if trying to salvage something from the wreck.

'Joseph Beavers, foyboatman; Robert Johnson, river-pilot; George Dobie, keelboatman; William Renshaw, foyboatman and Samuel Hawke, master's mate,' Anne read off her list.

'What's all this then?' asked Father Fletcher, pulling the ring of his Coke-can and sending Coke spurting across the court.

'We are trying to discover why that dog in the Priory attacks the turf of certain graves,' said Father da Souza with massive self-control.

'S'easy,' said Father Fletcher. 'Grass is always greener on the other side.' He buried his face in his Coke can and slurped pleasurably.

They finished their drinks in silence.

14

'By,' said Arthur, 'you have done well. That's what comes of Modern Thinking. Twenty pounds, eighty-eight pence!' He regarded the neat piles of silver and copper on the billiard-table with a near-Christmas delight. 'By, we can get a lot of paint wi' that.'

Anne stretched her aching back, pleased but exhausted. She'd been on the go since seven that morning, starting with the final dusting. Now it was seven in the evening. Timmo and Pat hadn't turned up. She wondered what had happened, but felt too tired to speculate.

The posters on the Castle railings had done their work. Ninety-seven people had signed the Watch House visitors' book. Seventy-two had bought her guidebooks. Everyone had asked endless questions. And the old wooden building, white in the sun, had baked them like an oven. Sweat had trickled down Anne's back as she talked. She had taken exactly ten minutes off at lunch, to drink a glass of cold milk. She'd been too excited to eat.

The first breeze of evening came, dry but refreshing. 'I'll close the windows,' she said.

'No,' said Arthur abruptly. Then added, 'Leave them, hinny. Let the place cool. I'll shut them after me supper. Go and enjoy yourself. Heeyar!' He gave her a tenpenny-piece out of his waistcoat pocket, with the grandeur of a rajah. He hadn't a clue about the cost of living, bless him. He gave his Navy pension straight to Prudie, and she bought his tobacco and socks.

Anne accepted the tenpence in the spirit intended, and went to change her T-shirt. She sat on her bed, weak with relief. It was all over. She had done her duty. She could forget the Watch House now.

Actually, the last three days hadn't been as bad as she'd feared. She had never had to be alone in the place. Timmo and Pat hadn't returned, but all kinds of people had turned up.

Mr McGill had come with the duplicated sheets of the guide-book, and his office stapler, striding up and down the rocket-room, nosing into this and that, and exploding into enthusiasm at intervals. Little old ladies had come to polish the brass, just like in church. The lads of the rocket-team, suddenly fired with new enthusiasm, had decided at the last minute to put on a demonstration of the breeches-buoy, and had spent hours fiddling with the rockets, drinking pint-pots of tea and singing incomprehensible songs. Even Prudie, relenting, had come to put the Hoover round. And they'd all made a fuss of her; taken guide-books away for their sons and married daughters, and nephews living in South Africa. Someone had even sent a reporter from the *Garmouth Weekly News*. The doings of Miss Anne were on everyone's lips. She was consulted on points of information frequently. There was talk of a petition in the town, to insist that the seawall be completed by the County Council, and the Watch House saved for posterity . . .

And every person who bustled in swept the Watch

133

House free of shadows. Why does everybody have this effect but me? Anne thought. Why is it only me that attracts the shadows?

But she had kept her word to the shadow. The Watch House was going to be saved and, even better, repainted as well. The Old Feller would rest contented now. He could go on making footsteps and knocking things over for ever and ever. Only she wouldn't have to be around to hear him.

She combed her hair and headed for Front Street and the open-air dancing that would end the Carnival. Dusk was falling blue over Garmouth, and the Carnival lights twinkled yellow and red. The breeze whispered through the long dry grass, carrying the sound of the Police Band playing *Puppet on a String*. Suddenly the world was so full of a faded childhood happiness that she wanted to cry.

But suddenly, perversely, the happiness the Carnival engendered turned her away from it. Close to, it wouldn't be so pretty; drunks, vulgar laughter, people eating chips out of paper bags. She'd had enough of crowds for one day. She didn't want any new thing to happen that might break her contentment. She turned away from the town, down the path to the North Pier.

Lots of people had had the same idea earlier. They were coming off the broad pier now, in family groups that parted, smiling, to let her through. The sunset was on their faces, and the darkening sea behind. They looked the way she felt: exhausted but happy. Little girls from the dancing-troupes, still vivid in purple and green, but trailing balloons and streamers limply now. Women from the vintage car-rally, with muslin scarves around their big hats. Men from the traction-engine rally, in oily Victorian overalls. Two youths from the model-flying display, dressed in Luftwaffe uniform and carrying a radio-controlled Messerschmitt. A hippy girl in long skirt and scarlet guardsman's tunic.

Strange, all the fancy-dress. It felt as if time itself was fraying, shaking loose. But nice, because everyone was smiling, squinting up their eyes against the sunset.

As she got further along the pier, and the sky darkened, the family groups thinned out. She passed through the last, and was alone. Except for one small person in Victorian top-hat and frock-coat, hurrying ahead of her towards the lighthouse. Head down and hands behind his back. Alone among the crowds he looked anxious. He kept peering over his shoulder at her, his face a white blur in the dusk. What part of the Carnival had he been in? He was too tidy for the traction-engines, and too early for the vintage cars.

The breeze grew colder, and Anne's arms went goosy. She wished she'd brought her cardigan. The little man was looking round so often, she felt compelled to imitate him. But there was nothing behind, except the last glimmer of sunset reflected in the ripples of the Gar.

When she looked to the front again, the dusk had deepened. The little man was no more than a flickering shadow. The light of the lighthouse began to flash. Its beams made a pale circling wheel overhead.

She felt an urge to be near him, in the loneliness of sea and sky. She walked faster, but she couldn't overtake him.

135

She was nearly at the pier-end now, where it broadened to encircle the lighthouse. The little man circled left and vanished. He didn't reappear. He must have stopped to peer out to sea, as people usually did.

Anne ran round the lighthouse.

He must be an art-student or something. The fancy-dress was so perfect. Tall rough beaver hat; baggy trousers over broad-stitched boots; wrinkled waistcoat with watch and chain. Arm resting a little proudly on a plaque set in the granite wall that read:

THIS PIER OPENED, 11 OCTOBER 1895

BY WILLIAM GRACE, MAYOR.

WILLIAM ARMSTRONG JOBLE, CONSULTING ENGINEER.

GEORGE TAYLOR AND SON, CONTRACTORS.

HENRY COOKSON, GAR IMPROVEMENT COMMISSION.

But those curling white whiskers weren't stuck on with theatrical gum. They were real. And that rose-bud mouth . . . she'd seen it somewhere before. And that nervous clenching of the hands . . .

Didn't she know him?

Of course not. It was just that he looked like that picture of Isambard Kingdom Brunel, who built the Great Western. Except Brunel had looked so much cockier with that big cigar. Not so scared . . .

And then she knew, quite certainly, that she was looking at a ghost. Because the light on the South Pier came on, and shone right through his face.

I am looking at a ghost, she thought, and I am not scared at all. Because it was the Old Feller, and she had done all the Old Feller had asked, and his face was kind.

136

'I . . .' she said foolishly and reached out a hand.

Then a horrible thing happened. The Old Feller's face began to fall apart with fear. The eyes screwed up. The mouth fell open in a soundless scream. As if she, Anne, were some kind of dreadful monster.

'It's me, Anne.' She took a step forward.

The ghost writhed away.

'Whatever's the matter?' Her own voice rose to a scared shriek.

This had happened before to her. Where? Where? In the orchard with Cousin Jane. She had walked towards Cousin Jane, and Jane had shrieked with terror. Because Anne, all unknowing, had had a spider in her hair, and Jane was terrified of spiders.

The Old Feller wasn't frightened of *her*. He was frightened of . . . Anne whirled round. Something faded round the curve of the lighthouse. Something red. There was a strong gust of seaweed; the smell of the bottom of a river.

Was it that hippy girl she'd seen, in the guardman's tunic, earlier? Was the hippy girl spying on her?

She ran after the blur of red tunic, angry with the rage that follows shock. Round the lighthouse she ran, with her fists clenched.

Nothing. She came round to the stone plaque again, and ran on. Round and round till she was panting. She tried doubling back. Nothing.

The Old Feller was gone. She was alone with something red that stank of the river and had terrified a ghost. She remembered the frantic writing in the dust.

An help An help.

She pressed herself against the curving wall of the lighthouse, and knew she dared not leave it, dared not venture the long lonely pier walk to safety and home. She could not see the red thing, but the deep-rotting smell of the river came and went.

Far off across the water, under the red and yellow points of light, the Garmouth Police Band struck up with *We'll gather lilacs in the Spring again.*

The lighthouse was automatic. The green door in its base was padlocked. A man came to see to it once a week. Arthur had told her.

She was half a mile from the nearest human face. Half a mile walk up the pier in the dark . . .

She might have stayed there for ever. But, away up the pier, she saw something flicker. A little worried figure in a beaver hat. The figure beckoned. Urgently, frantically. Wanting her to come.

With a sigh, she followed blindly, on legs that moved like alien levers.

The urgent flicker stayed with her, fifty yards ahead, until she met a bunch of men rolling down from Front Street, singing more incomprehensible songs and swigging out of bottles of beer.

As she ran past the Watch House, she saw the windows were still open. She burst into Brigade Cottage, saw Arthur sitting with his stockinged feet up, and shouted angrily:

'You haven't shut those windows.'

'Aye,' said Arthur placidly. 'Aah'll go and shut them, now Aah've had me supper.'

'You left those windows open?' said Prudie, sharply.

'Aye, well, he likes to hear the band, Carnival night.'

138

'You stupid old fool.'
'It's his Carnival. He started it, didn't he?'
Arthur walked off, whistling.

PART THREE

What the hammer? what the chain?
In what furnace was thy brain?
What the anvil? what dread grasp
Dare its deadly terrors clasp?

When the stars threw down their spears,
And water'd heaven with their tears,
Did he smile his work to see?
Did he who made the Lamb make thee?

W. Blake

15

Arthur picked up the last lollystick off the rocket-room floor. 'These modern bairns has no manners. Don't know what their parents teach 'em.'

'We forgot to put out litter-bins,' said Anne, leaning on her broom. Timmo and Pat might at least have come to help with the cleaning up.

'Litter-bins? We had no litter-bins when Aah was a lad. We kept our rubbish in our pockets, till we came to a dustbin. And their parents are no better. Look at those fag-ends.' But he was in a good mood really. Thinking of all the cut-price paint he could buy. So Anne took her chance.

'Arthur, what was the Old Feller's real name?'

Arthur pushed back his cap and scratched his head. 'Coxly or Coxhead or summat. Aah can't rightly say. Aah was about one year old when he died. 1903 that was. Ye'd have to ask one of the *old* Brigade members. Like Bosun Mason. Bosun was the one found him dead.' His eye brightened. 'Would ye like to meet Bosun? He's fond of company. He doesn't get about much these days.'

'How old is *he*?'

Arthur considered, head on one side.

'Ninety-six next birthday.'

'Come in, young Arthur,' said Bosun Mason. 'And

the young lady. Aah've been expecting you round for a crack. What's kept you?'

Arthur explained about the Watch House and the Carnival. He suffered a long interrogation about which objects had been moved, polished or replaced, and who had moved, polished and replaced them.

Then another interrogation about who was dead, who was dying, and who wasn't looking very well. Bosun Mason turned to Anne, and laid a huge mottled hand on her thigh with the privilege of the ancient.

'Aah'm the oldest left. Aah've outlived them all. Even the young'uns Aah taught to tie their first knot. All gone. Aah'll outlive young Arthur here, won't Aah, Arthur?'

Arthur grinned with adolescent embarrassment.

'Aah'm hanging on for me Telegram. Queen always sends a Telegram, when ye're a hundred. Saying "Well done", like. Only one thing worries me. Aah can't work out how the Queen knows when to *send* the telegram. How does she know who's dead or alive? D'you know, hinny?'

Anne had to admit she didn't. But Bosun wasn't bothered.

'Aah've worked out me plans. Aah give young Arthur here five shilling. When Aah'm ninety-nine, he can send the Queen a telegram. So she'll know in good time. And Aah've given two other young fellers five shillings, in case Arthur drops down dead afore then.'

Having settled the matter to his own satisfaction, he appeared to fall asleep. Anne went on studying him, as she had for the last half-hour, with complete awe. She had always thought of the old as frail. Bosun was far from frail. He fitted his armchair as snugly as an egg; partly because of the clothes he wore. Open overcoat, two open jackets, waistcoat and at least two jumpers. The whole topped-off with a woollen scarf wrapped round and round his neck. Layer on layer of fabric. Above, layer upon layer of Bosun. He was the most wrinkled man Anne had ever seen. The wrinkles under his eyes, descending, criss-crossed the wrinkles ascending from his mouth. Even the larger wrinkles were minutely wrinkled in turn. Only his mottled bald head was smooth; and the knuckles of the great hands that grasped a stick held upright before him. You couldn't even say he looked old; he had the agelessness of an elephant or tortoise.

'This is Miss Anne,' said Arthur loudly, with a trace of nervousness. 'Miss Fiona McGuire's daughter. Miss Fiona McGuire as was. Mrs Fiona Melton, now. Aah don't suppose you remember her?'

The tortoise eyes opened, and swivelled balefully on Arthur.

''Course Aah remember Miss Fiona. Aah remember her Dad, young McGuire. Owned three trawlers, back before the Depression. 1922 it was. The *Bright Adventure*, the *Bright Queen* and the *Bright Mermaid*. Good boats in their day. Aah remember Aah had words once wi' the skipper of the *Bright Queen*. Two boxes of fish he sold me short. Aah telled him to make the fish up, or Aah'd throw him in the Gut. He argued so long Aah throwed him into the Gut and walked away. Aah couldn't spare the time. Aah had six bairns to keep.' Satisfied, his eyes closed again.

'Miss Anne wrote that guide-book to the Watch

House Aah was telling you about. She's interested in the Old Feller.'

Now the eyes swivelled on Anne. She held their gaze with difficulty. Someone who called her dead grandfather 'young McGuire'. It was like looking in the face of God.

'Did you put the Old Feller in your guidebook?'

'No. I didn't know who he was.'

'Ah, that's wicked, them not telling you. Aah don't know what young folk are coming to today.' He gave Arthur a look that had him wriggling. 'The Old Feller was a great man. The greatest man Aah've ever known. But once you're dead, no matter how great you been, people forget ye. They nearly forget ye when ye're still alive, once ye're past ninety.'

Arthur wriggled again. Bosun closed his eyes.

'What did the Old Feller *do*?' asked Anne rather shrilly.

'Aah was *coming* to that. What *didn't* he do? He founded the Life Brigade, that's all. Oh, you won't find his name much in books, or on foundation stones. You need the help of mayors, you see, and the only way you can pay mayors back is to let them lay foundation stones. But it was Henry Cookson was the first secretary and raised the money. And it was Henry Cookson who was the first captain of the Brigade. Aah mind when Aah first saw him in action. Aah were only a bairn, clinging to me ma's skirts. But we all ran to the Watch House when we heard the maroon go. Middle of the night. A Russian full-rigged ship. The *Talinn* out of Riga. Hard on the Black Middens, just below the Watch House. South-east gale. The Brigade got a rocket aboard at the

146

third shot, but the crew didn't know what to do, being Russkies. They fixed the line too low, an' the first Russky was washed out of the breeches-buoy. The Brigade were at their wit's end, because the *Talinn's* foremast had gone overboard, and was beating the hull to bits. Aah'll never forget the noise it made, long as Aah live. Like a great drum!

'Anyway, Henry was off wi' his oilskins, and shinning hand over hand down the breeches-buoy. Everyone thought he was a gonner, but he made it. God's hand was on him that night. They saved every soul bar the first that drowned.

'Henry got the Royal Humane Society's Medal for that – and a medal from the Empress of Russia, all writ in Russian – ye'll have seen that down the Watch House. And Aah vowed that when Aah was a man, Aah'd join the Brigade. Aah've been a member seventy-eight year come Christmas.'

Bosun held back his many layers of clothing, with something of the coyness of a stripper. Underneath, still round his waist, he wore a white webbing belt marked GVLB. Only a bit greasy round the edges.

'Henry Cookson taught me all Aah know about saving life at sea. A fine man, but a driven one. Driven beyond reason. He was always on the go, as if something was after him. Us lads would often ask him out for a pint. But he could never be easy. He always had something else to do . . . about saving lives at sea.

'When Aah was young, he was a ship-owner. Inherited from his da. Fine house in Dockwray Square. Lovely wife and three bairns. All a man could wish. But he lived for nowt but the Brigade. Then he got crazed we should have piers at the mouth of the

147

Gar so ships wouldn't get wrecked on the Middens at all. Cookson's Folly, folks called it. But when they were built, the folk who'd laughed were glad.

'But it took all his time. Business went to pot. Wife ran off wi' another feller. Had to sell his ships. Had to go in lodgings wi' the money he had left. But still it was the Brigade. He was getting old, but he didn't care. Soaked to the skin many a time. Then he got that rheumatic fever and his heart went bad. No more, says the doctor. We didn't see him for a bit.

'Then one night we got a paddle-steamer ashore on Battery Rocks; that's on the seaward side o' the Middens. It weren't a bad wreck, just long, and awkward on account of it was full of silly women who wouldn't stop screaming and carrying on. Captain couldn't handle them, so three of us lads went across. Aah knocked one fat wife senseless, and we loaded her into the buoy, and we had no more bother.

'Anyway, just on dawn, we got the last wife ashore; not a soul lost. We were all sitting supping tea wi' plenty o' rum in it, and every feller was shouting did yer see *this* and did yer see *that*. Really meaning had Aah noticed how brave *they'd* been personally. When little Tommy Scase leans forwards and taps me on the knee, sly-like. Did Aah know we had a visitor? he says. Where? Aah says. Yonder under the billiard-table, in the shadows, he says. A half-grown kid crept in to spy on us, like young lads do.

'Well, we was all a bit jolly, like, what wi' the success an' the rum. So Aah dives under the billiard-table shouting, "Come out, you little monkey, Aah've twigged yer." Aah grabs him by the arm, and he was stiff and stark. All hunched in the corner wi' his hands over his face.

' "Oh, God help us," Aah ses.

' "What you got there, Bosun?" ses Tommy Scase.

' "One for the mortuary," Aah ses.

' "Drag him out an let's see who he is," ses Tommy.

'So Aah dragged him out, but Aah couldn't make out who he was, wi' his hands over his face. "Aah can't move them," Aah ses. "Aah'm scared o'breaking his arms."

' "Never heed," ses Tommy. "He won't hold it against ye now."

'Aah wish Aah'd never moved those hands. It was upsetting enough finding it was the Old Feller. But the look on his face. Aah never saw worse in the trenches in the Great War.

'We carried him out to our mortuary. All the lads was blubbin' a bit, an' they'd seen their share o' drowned men. Aah said Aah'd stay wi' him, till the rigor mortis passed off. It took twenty hours to pass. Aah straightened his body, but Aah could never straighten his face. When the doctor came, he said it was nowt – just a spasm of the heart-attack that killed him. But Aah could tell the doctor was just saying that to cheer himself up.

'Aye, it were a shame. Aah loved that man like he was my own Da . . .'

The Bosun closed his eyes. One old man's tear started down his cheek, and got lost among the wrinkles.

Anne managed to clear her throat on the third attempt.

'Is there a picture of the Old Feller in the Watch House?'

''Course there is,' said the Bosun, creaky with self-engendered emotion. 'The lads clubbed together on his last birthday and took him to Mundy's the Photographers, to have his portrait took. We even took him a cork life-jacket to wear . . .'

He closed his eyes again; there was a slight snore.

'Leave him,' said Arthur. 'He's wore out his strength.'

They tiptoed out together.

16

That afternoon, Anne slipped up to see Corporal Rollo. She had a lot of thinking to do. And at least *he* couldn't tell her she was mad.

Even in the sunlight, now, she was jumpy about red things seen out of the corner of her eye. But Garmouth Priory on a Sunday afternoon was too much for any ghost. It was crowded with trippers. Scholarly elderly men, with binoculars hung over their floral beach-shirts, paced up and down in pairs, outdoing each other with comments about passing ships and Saxon kings. Children leapt and screamed over the tombs in pursuit of beachballs. A fat lady had settled herself and her two children by Corporal Rollo, and said alternately:

'Leave your sister *alone*, Simon,' and,

'Stop *provoking* him, Marlene.'

The children continued their sibling strife as if she was no more than a bumblebee.

Perhaps it was only the noise of the children, but Anne felt completely desperate.

The ghosts were outside the Watch House now. They could appear to her any time, anywhere. And she knew it could only get worse.

She could lurk inside Brigade Cottage and never go out. But that would slowly screw her up till she really went mad.

She could write to Mother; and suffer the attentions of the ever-present Monty, for ever and ever, amen.

She could tell Prudie everything that happened and be wheeled off to the doctor's. But he would only give her a little talk on the growing-pains of adolescence and a small prescription for valium.

Besides, she still felt an unreasoning concern for the Old Feller. It would be cowardly just to run away and leave him.

Help An Help An Help

She had thought it was help for the Watch House he meant, but she was wrong.

The Old Feller hadn't run out on the Russkies when they needed *him*.

Running away was *always* wrong.

If only she had some help. But who would believe in a nice ghost haunted by a nasty ghost? By a ghost who threw things with terrible violence, and smelled of the bottom of the river.

Something red.

'There you are,' said a voice. All her limbs flew around in a helpless panic.

'*Steady,*' said the voice. Someone sat down beside her. It was Timmo. 'Prudie said you'd be here. Where've you been hiding yourself all the week?'

'I've been busy,' she said aggressively, 'with the Watch House for the Carnival. I thought you were going to help.' She couldn't disguise the sudden spurt of anger.

'Pat's had a virus. She's still in bed with it. She was worried that you hadn't been round to see her. She rang me up last night and asked me to look you up. She thought you'd call . . .'

152

So Pat hadn't just walked out on her, after all. The sudden relief made it impossible to keep the tears back, fight though she might. Why did she always *expect* people to let her down?

'Oh, God,' said Timmo. 'You thought . . . sorry. It's my fault. Only I got involved in an argument with a kid who builds kites and I've been experimenting like mad. I'm sorry. I always leave the human relationships bit to Pat. I suppose I'm pretty awful, really. If it wasn't for Pat I wouldn't have any friends.'

He sounded so abjectly woebegone that she had to smile and say, 'Cheer up!'

He cheered up with quite indecent haste. 'How'd the Carnival day go, then?'

'Oh, fine.' There was a listlessness in her voice that made him look at her sharply.

'What else has happened?'

'Oh, leave it. You'll just think me a crazy female.'

'More bother at the Watch House?'

She nodded.

He said, 'Actually, I don't think you are a crazy female. I know I was snotty about that lighthouse spouting Morse Code, but it was really Pat I was being snotty with. It's the one thing I can't stand about her. Horoscopes, ouija-boards, telling fortunes by tea-leaves, spiritualism – she's hooked on them all. She ought to grow up.'

Anne suppressed her usual urge to gloat over someone else being criticized. 'Everyone's got funny little ways.'

'Yeah,' said Timmo, with a rueful grin. 'Anyway, tell Uncle Timothy all about it.'

She told him everything.

153

After she'd finished he said:

'*Ware Hague*. Sounds like a telly advert. Wear Brutus Jeans. Don't be vague – ask for Haig.' Then he was silent a long time.

'Do you think I'm going mad?'

'No,' he said at last. 'If only for one reason. When that glass tumbler got broken, the laws of physical reality got broken at the same time. That great gouge out of the window-frame. Nobody could have thrown the tumbler *that* hard. So if we have one breach in physical reality, why not more? Who am I to pick and choose?'

'If I was going ... peculiar,' said Anne, suddenly feeling a lot more cheerful, 'I don't think that would be the way I'd go. I'd just get more and more miserable.'

Another long silence.

'Actually,' said Timmo, 'there's one possible scientific explanation for ghosts ... some scientists are interested in it. The idea that strong emotions are a kind of energy and somehow indestructible. When something nasty's happened in a place, the place may hold the vibes, a bit like a tape-recorder. Maybe for centuries. And some people – who these scientists call 'sensitives' – are able to pick up these vibes. Maybe the Old Feller did see something nasty once, at the end of the pier. Maybe he left a recording for you. It's a fascinating idea ... I wonder how we could investigate it. Fancy another shot at hypnotism?'

'I don't know,' she said doubtfully. His theory certainly fitted what had happened the last time she'd been hypnotized. The ghostly rocket-crew, ship, storm, oil-lamps were logical enough, explained as a

154

playback of the Old Feller's memories of the wreck of the *Talinn*. They tallied so completely with the Bosun's description.

But psychic tape-recorders didn't throw glass tumblers, or write in the dust of the present day . . .

An Help. An Help. Help.

'OK, we'll try hypnotism,' she said.

She immediately became Timmo's most prized possession. He bought her an ice cream from the van parked by the Priory Gate; cracked his most preposterous jokes. He nodded at a tombstone representing a Greek Ionic column, dramatically broken off half-way up.

'Know what *that* guy died of?'

'What?'

'A fractured temple.'

'Oh?'

'Don't you get it? A fractured *temple*. Greek temples have columns like that. So . . . a broken column equals a fractured *temple*. Oh, why do I bother?'

But she wasn't listening. Behind that column, a lettered stone was set into the ruined wall of the Priory.

IN GRATEFUL MEMORY OF
MAJOR SCOBIE HAGUE
LATE OF HER MAJESTY'S 55TH
REGT OF FOOT WHO DROWNED
WHILE ATTEMPTING THE MERCY
OF RESCUE 14TH OCTOBER 1854
THIS STONE WAS ERECTED BY
HIS CHILDHOOD SWEETHEART
AND HIS GRIEVING FRIENDS.

Timmo walked forward and peered at it.

'Curious. It's a genuine wall-plaque – not a tomb-stone moved from elsewhere. And no mention of *near this spot lies the body of* like they sometimes have. A strong case for *ne habeas corpus* – we never found the body. Poor old Major Hague, in his brave scarlet coat . . .'

The message screamed through Anne's mind in its scrawling letters.

'Timmo,' she whispered. 'Timmo. That thing . . . on the pier . . . had a scarlet coat. It's *him*.'

Next morning, Timmo had to bully her all the way up the hill to Front Street. If he hadn't called for her, she would never have got out of bed. Her legs felt like lead; she had hardly slept.

Front Street, full of shoppers and red double-decker buses, was insubstantial, like a dream. It was the real world that was ghostly now.

They got on a bus. Timmo said something to the conductor and paid the fares. Then he returned to the attack.

'Look, Anne, it could all be nothing. Maybe Hague got drowned in India or something. That would be an excellent reason why they had no body to bury. Besides, Hague's far too early to have anything to do with the Old Feller. The Old Feller must've been only about ten when *this* Hague drowned.'

'How'd you know that?' she flared suddenly, out of her quaking inertia.

'Found out the same place we're going to this morning: the back-copies section of the *Garmouth*

Weekly News. It goes back to 1830. The Old Feller, or more correctly, Henry Cookson, was born in 1844.'

They obviously knew Timmo of old at the *Garmouth News*. The lady in the front office, who did the adverts and the lost-and-found, motioned him through to the back premises with a flick of her head, without even pausing in writing out a small ad for a second-hand billiard-table.

The reporter in the back premises, a hungry-looking balding man with open waistcoat and rimless spectacles, groaned and said, 'Oh, God, not you again.' The he got up, pulled back his chair, and hauled up a trapdoor in the floor. He pressed a switch, and a faint yellow light lit the descending stone steps.

'You know 1941's no good – they were blown up in the Blitz?'

'Yes,' said Timmo patiently.

'And it's no good looking for 1893 and 1894 . . .'

'Because you had a flood in the cellar and they happened to be on the bottom . . .' said Timmo wearily.

'Correct,' said the reporter. 'Just as long as you know. Knock on the trapdoor when you've found what you want.'

They went down the steps. Anne heard the trapdoor close behind them, and the reporter drag his chair back into place on top of it.

'Marvellous place this,' said Timmo with gusto. 'The Tutankhamun's Tomb of the Thomson Newspaper chain.'

Anne stared around her. Brick walls. Deep arches in the walls, full of flat, half-size coffins.

The nearest coffins were quite gay; bound in bright

157

red leather; their dates glittered golden from the spines. 1975; 1974; 1973. The 1960 ones were rosy pink with dust. The 1950s were a fading hope, and the 1930s were a withered brown.

Timmo gave a Tarzan-like whoop, and headed for the darkest corner, where 1850 was scrawled on the bricks with chalk. He crouched near the floor, bony backside stuck far into the air, and his head thrust into an arch, where the torchlight outlined his unruly hair like a halo.

'Fifty-one . . . fifty-two . . . damn, fifty-six . . . some-one's been messing about. Fifty-five . . . ah, fifty-four. Give me a hand, Anne.'

Anne knelt beside him. She couldn't think straight any more; dumb obedience was all she could manage. Damp soaked up into the knees of her denims from the stone flagstones. She brushed cobwebs from her face. The smell of dust was overpowering. If I ever get out of this, she thought, *if* I ever get out of this, I shall never open a history-book again. History in books is a lie. Reading about Castlereagh and Wellington is a lie; because what you read is printed on nice clean shiny new paper. *Real* history is damp and dust and cobwebs and dead people who won't lie down. I shall do English, Needlework and Domestic Science at 'A' level, and marry a scientist, and live in a dustfree house with Swedish furniture and stainless steel. And use the Hoover every day . . .

'Come on,' hissed Timmo. 'Make an effort. It takes two to lift these bloody things.'

She made an effort, and they dragged the volume for 1854 out into the middle of the stone floor. Timmo heaved back the front cover with a loud crack, and began turning pages. She held the torch for him with shaky fingers. Each page was torn in the middle at the bottom. Where people put their hand to lift it. The paper must be terribly frail . . . Each page was white in the middle, but darker brown round the edges; almost like a great flat mushroom. The pages gave off a mushroomy smell.

August. September. October. October 6th. October 13th. October 20th. . . It was a funny looking newspaper. Six columns of tiny print to every page. No photographs, or even big drawings. Just little wood-engravings – a coach and horses in full gallop here (advertising a newly-started stage-coach run to London); a Royal Coat of Arms there (advertising the opening of a County Court Session). All the adverts jammed in higgledy-piggledy with the news.

'Hey,' said Timmo, with high delight. 'Look!'

Her heart gave a great jump, but it was only an advert.

THEATRE ROYAL, GARMOUTH
THIS DAY SATURDAY OCTOBER 29TH 1854
COMMENCING AT HALF PAST TWO O'CLOCK
MONSTER EQUESTRIAN AND GYMNASTIC
ENTERTAINMENT
TURPIN'S RIDE TO YORK
CONCLUDING WITH, BY OVERWHELMING
DEMAND
AND POSITIVELY FOR THE LAST TIME
THE DEATH OF BLACK BESS .

'Interesting, that,' said Timmo. 'Not *Dick* Turpin's ride to York, like we say. Just *Turpin's* ride to York.'

She could have hit him. How could he be so detached and cheerful?

But just at that moment, he said, 'Oh, oh!'

And there was the headline.

APPALLING CATASTROPHE – LOSS OF *HOPLITE*. The headline was only a quarter of an inch high, but there were three whole columns of report.

'Let's get it upstairs,' said Timmo. 'We can't read this print down here. We'll ruin our eyes.'

He hammered on the trapdoor, the reporter's chair scraped back, and they staggered with their burden into the light of day.

'Is the young lady all right?' asked the reporter. 'Nasty, unhealthy place that. Never go down, meself.'

He showed them to an empty desk, just across a hardboard partition from the lady who was doing the small-ads. Anne could hear her voice quite clearly.

'Now, hinny, was it a *large* dog? Black with white spots and a white end to its tail? Answers to "Bessy" . . .'

She began to read, following Timmo's dirty finger. The printing was so tiny. How had they managed to read it with only oil-lamps and candles? And all the time the lady next door droned on with comforting trivia about three-piece suites in excellent condition. Cut or uncut moquette . . .

APPALLING CATASTROPHE – LOSS OF *HOPLITE*.
Last month we praised the sea-going qualities of the Gar-built steamship Hoplite, whose passages to Australia have so outmatched the long line of clippers that hail from the great port of Liverpool. This week

it is our painful duty to give details of her entire destruction, involving frightful loss of life.

On Tuesday last, the greatest satisfaction was experienced by many anxious hearts in Garmouth when the telegraph announced that the Hoplite was at Hull – fifty-eight days from Melbourne – and that she might be looked for in Garmouth in a few hours. A few passengers landed at Hull, but the great majority stuck to the good ship which had brought them so happily from the Antipodes. But alas! that journey was to terminate in destruction of the noble ship and a watery grave for eighty-seven people within a hundred yards of land.

After she passed Hartlepool at half past four p.m. a strong breeze from the ENE sprang up. The wind began to go more to the east and increase in strength. At ten o'clock, being near high water and the atmosphere being thick with rain, the wind blew that hurricane from the SE which has proved so disastrous all along the British coast. The vessel was put under all steam and left with bare poles. On entering the estuary of the Gar, finding the vessel had got too near the north shore, an effort was made to put her about. But the gale was so furious that the small strength of her propeller and the height of her masts and upper gear rendered the attempt futile and they could not get her round.

Finding they were nearing and nearing the shore, the port anchor was let go in sixteen fathoms. Before this, rockets and blue lights had been sent up in the hope of attracting the pilot, but all in vain. The weather was so thick and dark that nothing could be seen.

161

At two o'clock on Wednesday she parted her anchor-chain. The ship having got entangled with the rocks and struck stern-on, the main-mast was cut away at half past two, and in going over the side carried the mizzen-top with it, with a fearful crash. It is said that an axe for the purpose was not readily available in the excitement, but that one was not necessary, for in cutting the stays, so strong was the gale that the mast toppled over the side at once. But the remedy was too late. Heeling at the storm she swung her broadside to land.

At about four o'clock, the waves beating against her broadside with continued violence, she suddenly snapped asunder amidships and tumbled in pieces like a house of cards. All the passengers save one had been kept below, chiefly in the saloons, as they had been repeatedly assured by Captain Taylor that there was no immediate danger. The falling machinery and lumber seemed to bury fifty of the wretched people. It is believed that large numbers were actually killed by the crashing debris, but soon afterwards the whole ship was broken up like a shattered bottle.

The scenes abroad during the last hour were painful beyond description. Wives and husbands, children and parents, lovers and friends were embracing each other with the consciousness that they were about to meet inevitable death. The Rev. Mr Hodge, a clergyman from New Zealand, before this, had commenced a prayer-meeting in the saloon, which was earnestly participated in by many until the flooding of water rendered panic universal.

On the vessel breaking up, numbers of people could be seen by the ghastly light of the full moon, floating

162

about for a few minutes. But with the strength of the waves, the mass of debris which thickly covered the sea and struck many a brave and struggling man's brains out, few were able to gain a firm hold on the land. Many were washed on and off the shelving rocks several times, and many who thought they had secured land, or held fast by a jutting rock were hurled back again, into a watery grave.

At eight o'clock in the morning, nothing but corpses left on the sand revealed the terrible catastrophe that had befallen nearly a hundred beings, a few hours before glowing with joy at once again sighting the shores of Old England, for which they had toiled and saved.

The Black Middens, where the vessel had made her end, are rocks of a peculiar character, most antagonistic to an iron vessel. The limestone is sharp, irregular and as rough as a file where not covered with sea weed. Yesterday, pieces of sheet-iron, doubled up like tin, and fragments of machinery strewed the beach. At low water, some of the remnants of the engine-room could be discerned, and an irregular mass of sheet-iron said to be the stern.

Up to Thursday, eighty-six bodies had been recovered, including those of the captain and the superior officers. They were dreadfully mangled in most cases, either by the sharp rocks or the falling iron-work. One body had the head completely off, though the neck and lower chin remained. They were mostly only partly-dressed, indeed some were nearly in a state of nudity, their clothes having been torn off by contact with the rocks. The body of a female picked up was so jammed in between some rocks that some considerable force was required to extricate it. The bodies were spread out in Garmouth church for identification. One body, which a crowd was mournfully following, on enquiry turned out to be that of a Garmouth man, Anthony Beavers, who had been washed away by the hungry waves while attempting the mercy of rescue.

On Thursday, on the strand, a waistcoat was picked up, containing a gold watch. Some sovereigns were also picked up, together with a box that had contained gold, which was addressed 'to the Union Bank, London'.

The sole survivor was a Portuguese seaman named Joseph Rogerson, and he managed to get ashore more through Providence than design or ability. At the height of the storm, but before the vessel was fully broken, Captain Taylor called for volunteers to swim ashore with a light line, in the hope of setting up a breeches-buoy. Rogerson was chosen from the many willing, together with Major Hague of the 55th Regiment of Foot, returning to his home town after lately serving in Australia. Major Hague was a man of gigantic stature and noted for his formidable prowess as a swimmer throughout the Antipodes. Even when faced with such Herculean peril, he refused to be parted from an item of his luggage. He said it contained the thing most precious to his heart. As he was soon to be married, the other thing most precious to his heart lay sleeping in the town, and he hoped, ere daybreak, to lay the one in the lee of the other. Such light-hearted courage, in the midst of peril, heartened all those listening.

Major Hague's luggage was lashed to a massive

164

spar, and both men jumped with it into the waves. They availed to stay together to within yards of the shore. Twice Rogerson heard Major Hague cry out, "There is hope yet." But within the sound of breakers they were parted by a capricious wave that swept Rogerson up the Gar to where it curved southward, and the loom of the south shore broke the fury of the waves.

After daybreak, Rogerson was rescued by two foy-boatmen from the shallows of Jarrow Slake, being too overcome to bring himself to shore.

The body of Major Hague has to date not been recovered. It is to be presumed that he perished in his heroic attempt; at the time the storm was so great that any attempt at rescue was attended by the greatest peril.

The morning after the disaster, Captain Mends immediately despatched a steam-launch of man-o-war's men to guard the wreck, though a furious gale was still blowing at the time. The Coast Guard, together with a party of the Northumbrian Militia from Newcastle, were also summoned to the scene to prevent looting and plunder, should such a disposition be shown.

'There you are,' said Timmo cheerfully. 'Old Hague was a hero, who died performing the mercy of rescue, as they so quaintly put it. So why should he turn into a nasty ghost who throws things?'

Anne wasn't listening; she was thinking.

A man of gigantic stature. Drowned on the Middens and never found. A scarlet tunic. A skull of exceptional size and strength; found by fishermen on the Middens and kept in the glass cabinets of the billiard-room.

And the name *Hoplite*. When she'd been rescued by Arthur, when she had nearly drowned on the Middens, when she had gone down and down into the dark, she had thought of a ship's name. Only she had thought it was *Hop Light*. The *Hoplite* drifting off Van Diemen's Land . . . which was in Australia . . .

It all fitted together.

'You can leave that,' said the reporter, nodding to the bound editions of the *Garmouth Weekly News* for 1854. 'We've got somebody else coming in to see that this afternoon. They rang up this morning. Funny, you aren't asked for something for donkey's years, then you're asked for it twice in the same day. But it often happens.'

Now it was Timmo's turn to flare up.

'Who is it? Who wants to see it?'

'Vicar-feller. That Catholic one, I think.'

'Father da Souza?'

'Some funny name like that. Seemed very interested in a drowning accident. Funny tastes people have. You'd think we had enough troubles in the twentieth century.'

'But . . .' said Anne.

'He's spying on you!' shouted Timmo, completely losing his cool for once. 'Da Souza. He was in the Priory yesterday afternoon, with a pair of binoculars. Said he was bird-watching. But I pointed out a kittiwake and said it was a gannet, and he took it like a lamb. Oh, I had a right laugh, I can tell you. I can't stand that pair. Fletcher's bad enough, but he's just

166

thick. Da Souza's got brains, which makes it all the more revolting.'

'But . . .'

'He's got a nose for misery, that one. He's after you for a convert. You wouldn't be the first convert he's made. My mother says . . .'

But Anne wasn't listening. From somewhere had come the tiniest breath of hope.

17

'Timothy Jones, you're *mad*!' said Pat. She was sitting up in bed, colour flaring in her cheeks. She thumped the sheets and blankets with ineffectual hands. 'You are *not* going to hypnotize Anne again. She's lost half a stone in weight. She jumps at the least noise like a scared rabbit. What are you trying to do, *kill* her? If you don't promise not to hypnotize her, I'm going to see your father!'

'What you expect her to do then?' yelled Timmo. 'Sit round waiting for the next thing to happen? That *would* drive her nuts. When you're in a corner, attack. That's what I say.'

Pat's mother put her head round the bedroom door. Her face showed slight concern, worry, overlaid with a thin veneer of tolerance and understanding parental liberalism. 'More tea, anybody?'

'No thanks, Mum.'

'No thanks, Mrs Pierson.'

'Sorry about the row,' said Timmo. 'We were just arguing.'

'I'd noticed,' said Mrs Pierson. 'Well, if you're sure there's nothing . . .'

'No, thank you.'

'No, thank you.'

'No, thanks.'

Mrs Pierson withdrew with a certain reluctance.

'Actually, I want to be hypnotized again,' said Anne. 'I can't stand much more of these goings on. I thought we might try once more, and then if nothing changes for the better I'd go . . .'

'To London, to your mother?' asked Pat.

'Yes,' said Anne. She had been going to say, 'Father da Souza.' But on second thoughts there was no point in upsetting Timmo at this stage.

'Oh, Anne, is it *wise*?' Pat took Anne's hand in both of hers, her eyes shining with slightly-tearful affection. But Pat's affection just strengthened Anne's determination. The Old Feller was *alone*. He didn't even have someone who cared, like Pat.

'Then I'm coming with you,' said Pat.

'But you're *ill*,' said Timmo.

'See how fast I can get well,' said Pat. 'I feel better already.'

Timmo finished his milkshake. 'I thought it all out. Lying in bed this morning. The thing that frightened you the last time was losing contact with Pat and me. Feeling so *alone*. But if I hypnotize you here, before we get within a mile of the Watch House, *I* can dictate what goes on. I can tell you to go on holding my hand and Pat's, whatever happens. And I can tell you that you can talk to me and Pat, and hear our voices, whatever happens. That means we'll have no more of this cliff-top wrestling – I'm not built for it. And if you get too scared, just squeeze my hand twice, and I'll clap my hands and get you straight out of it.'

'You can't hypnotize me here,' said Anne, glancing round the ice cream parlour. 'Mr Antonioni wouldn't like it.'

169

'Mr Antonioni won't even notice. He's having his afternoon siesta standing up, like a horse.'

And indeed, the plump Italian was leaning on his counter, eyes shut, with the endless patience of a man who makes his living by awaiting other people's desires.

'Won't take a tick,' Timmo said. 'Got you used to it the last time.'

Six swings of that watch and chain and she was resting in that lovely state of childhood irresponsibility; enjoying the round-topped marble tables with their curving gilt legs and faces peering out of the cast-iron foliage. And the bead of perspiration running down Mr Antonioni's nose; and the glint of sun on the glass and brass of ice cream machines.

They crept into the Watch House like thieves. But Prudie's kitchen-curtain still twitched once; and Arthur waved from where he was mowing grass further along the cliff. It was a comfort. In a funny way, Prudie and Arthur would be with her, as well as Pat and Timmo. If only Father Fletcher and Father da Souza had been sunbathing and arguing on the grass . . . And the Old Feller. He must know she was coming to help. But she was still shivering, in spite of the heat. In spite of the knowledge that she was doing the right thing.

They drew up three of the old armchairs. Anne wriggled herself into some kind of comfort. She let Pat clasp her right hand with a grip like a vice. Pat was using both her hands, as if she meant to hold Anne down by brute force. Timmo clasped her left hand in one of his. His hand felt hard and bony and

170

much more assuring than Pat's. There was so much *vitality* in Timmo.

The watch and chain dangled. An intense stillness returned to the rocket-room. Boards creaked in the heat of the sun; somewhere overhead a mouse was scampering. She could feel trickles of sweat between her hand and Pat's. Through the window, tiny triangles of wave followed each other endlessly along the blue bulk of the South Pier.

'Anything?' asked Timmo, after a long pause. *He* was holding her hand in both of his now.

'Nothing,' said Anne.

'Maybe the Old Feller's having a siesta, like Mr Antonioni!'

'Don't mock,' said Anne. She didn't feel scared any more. Felt very strong; part of an invading army, called Anne-Pat-Timmo. Perhaps too strong, too nosy. Too full of life. Too much for the Old Feller . . . C'mon, she thought tenderly, coaxingly. C'mon, we're all *kind*. We won't eat you. Trust us.

She felt soaked with sweat now. Swimmy with the heat.

Then total blackness, with the wind tearing. A pain in her left arm, and a pain in her chest. Legs walking and wobbling uncontrollably. Alone. Desperation. Terror. She crashed over something she couldn't see, and fell.

'Steady, girl,' said a familiar voice. Timmo's voice. Then she could feel four warm fierce hands, holding her own in the dark. That made it better. The terror and loneliness retired to a distance, though they didn't go away.

It was a funny feeling. As if she and Timmo and

171

Pat were inside a bus that was lost in the dark, with a frightened driver, and about to break down. Only the bus had legs, not wheels.

'What's happening?' hissed Timmo.

'He's fallen down in the dark. I can't see a thing. He's ill, I think. *Awful* pain in his arm and chest.'

'Sounds like angina,' said Timmo. 'Pretty fatal heart disease. This could be his last journey. The one where he died. D'you want to go on, or shall I clap my hands?'

'Going on. He's got up again. Oh, I can see lighted windows, very faint. I think it's the Watch House. He's trying to get up the hill to the Watch House.'

The Watch House windows got bigger. They swayed alarmingly, and swung off without warning to left or right. Three times they vanished as the Old Feller fell. The pains got worse. She could hear old lungs straining like leather bellows.

Then the Watch House door, banging in the wind. The Old Feller supported himself against the doorpost, then staggered on. Dragging footsteps loud on the floorboards.

The rocket-room, under its swaying oil-lamps, was empty of everything but shadows. Through the windows, further out along the cliff, she saw the sudden flare of a rocket.

The Old Feller groped to a chair and sat down. He felt little glows of pride as the rockets flared, and a lot of despair in between. He knew he couldn't make it any further. He would sit and wait for the Brigade to finish and come back to him.

Then, outside the window, at the furthest extent of the lamplight, Anne saw a faint patch of scarlet.

The scarlet from the pier.

A man was standing, looking in. A huge man in military tunic with braid on the shoulders. He was soaked, streaming water. Fair hair straggled down his red face. He held something under one arm. With the other, he beckoned the Old Feller to come outside.

The pain in the Old Feller's chest became so great that Anne cried out. Pain all over. A kind of silent screaming.

'Hey, Anne, you all right?' Timmo's voice, urgent.

'Get her out of it, for God's sake,' whispered Pat. 'Can't you feel – she's as stiff as a board. Get her out before she has a fit or something. *C'mon*, Timmo.'

Anne gasped, 'No.' It was all she could manage.

A change had come over the figure outside. The face above the tunic had gone dead white. The mouth hung open, slack.

Then one blue eye slimed, and ran down the cheek, leaving only a punctured bag of membrane. Then only a black empty socket. Then the other eye burst and descended, with agonizing slowness.

But the sockets went on staring.

Then a hand came up, grasped the mouth, and pulled it sideways like a curtain. Teeth and bone glinted. Everywhere, the face was shredding, falling in fragments of grey gibbet-meat, until only a skull with hair remained.

The tunic dissolved to tattered lace, without losing its scarlet.

And still the arm beckoned.

There was a whirl of furniture and doors and floorboards. The Old Feller was running from room to room. Then just blackness.

173

Was this the end? Had the Old Feller died? But the feeling of terror went on.

Slits of light. The kind you get when you peer through your fingers.

The Old Feller was in the billiard-room now, hunched under the table. Hiding his face in his hands, and yet unable to resist peeping. At the nearest window.

A head rose in that window, like a rising moon. The round white top of a skull. A thick powerful skull with strands of yellow hair still sticking to it.

Blackness again. Then the slits of fingers again.

The skull had rebuilt itself into a face. Then it began falling apart all over again. Somehow, to Anne, if not to the Old Feller, it was not quite so terrible the second time. Like seeing a horror movie second time round.

Blackness.

Then the blessed sight of Pat's healthy young unchanging cheeks.

They walked down to the little beach between the Watch House cliff and the Priory cliff. It was mainly occupied by the yacht club, but there were a few kids playing on the sand, and a few mums knitting and drinking tea out of thermos flasks, and an ice cream van to supply their needs. Timmo bought three large cones, with two chocolate-flake bars in each.

'Last of the big spenders,' said Pat with the rudeness of relief. She was still clinging on to Anne's hand, and Anne was vaguely wishing she wouldn't. 'It must have been *horrible* for you, Anne.'

But Anne wasn't feeling too horrible. She was

enjoying the ice cream and the sun and the screeching kids throwing buckets of sand at each other; sucking it all in like a medicine. She felt . . . convalescent.

'It was horrible, and yet it wasn't. Horrible for the Old Feller . . . nobody can say *how* horrible . . . but I had you and Timmo. I wasn't alone. And I knew that it was just the Old Feller playing back his memories of something that happened nearly a hundred years ago . . . and there was something else . . .'

'Yeah?' said Timmo eagerly.

'Well . . . it was when . . . Hague . . . began changing himself the second time around. It felt not so much horrible as . . . obscene. Like a dirty old man exposing himself in a park. I felt he did it over and over again . . . that he got some nasty kick out of it. I began . . . just began . . . to despise him . . . it. It turned him into a kind of . . . child's bogeyman. It could have ended up in a kind of dreary boredom. Like seeing a TV series, that you once thought great, for the seventh time.'

'*Once* would be too often for me,' said Pat with a great shudder, in which neither delight, nor envy were quite lacking.

'No,' said Timmo. 'It's fascinating. It's well . . . I don't want to build up your hopes too much, but it is *hopeful*. I don't know if all ghosts like frightening people . . . but what happens to the inside workings of a frightening kind of ghost when people start finding it a bore? I mean, does it start undermining the ghostly self-confidence? No, don't laugh – though I suppose we could *do* with a laugh just now – what happens to *you* when you lose self-confidence? At tennis, for instance?'

'I play very badly,' said Anne.

'And what are you but a ghost inside a solid body? That's what sickens me about nearly all the ghost-stories I've read. A ghost has only got to groan, or manifest, or clank some chains, and quite solid citizens start having panics all over the scene. Not realizing that they themselves are ghosts *plus*. I mean, maybe one human against one ghost is pretty dicey. But what about three humans against one ghost? Three humans who're good friends – who work as a team.'

Anne finished her ice cream briskly. 'Let's go back and try again.'

'Oh, Anne,' wailed Pat. 'You *couldn't*.'

'I *could*. There's a lot we don't know yet – a lot more the Old Feller can tell us. If he will. And the more we know . . .'

'That's a girl,' said Timmo, enthusiastically.

They went up the cliff, very close together. They did not look like a beaten army.

18

'Hey,' came Timmo's voice anxiously. 'You all right?'

''Course I'm all right,' whispered Anne. 'Don't talk so much.' Which was rather hard on Timmo. How could he know how snug she suddenly felt?

She was lying in a bed, under a patchwork quilt. In a marble fireplace a fire was burning, low but cheerful. By its glow she could see wonderful things. A full-rigged model ship, all of three feet long, on the mantelpiece. A model paddle-steamer on a side table. It had its deck off, and she could see the firelight glinting on its brass boiler and three brass funnels.

The walls of the room were white-panelled and hung with charts. A great wind was blowing outside. Long red velvet curtains moved in the draughts. But it only made the room feel more safe, more secure.

Then, far off, there was a little explosion. Immediately, she felt the Old Feller leap with excitement. He wriggled under the bedclothes, as if trying to make up his mind. Twice he put his bare feet to the floor, and then drew them back into bed again. Finally he got up and reached for his breeches and waistcoat. Then the tweed greatcoat and flat cap, hung behind the door.

How huge everything seemed. Even the table with the paddle-steamer came up nearly to the Old Feller's chin. Surely they didn't have *such* huge furniture in

Victorian times? Then she realized. The Old Feller was just a little boy. A little boy about ten years old. He opened the bedroom door silently, boots in hand; slid into a corridor lit by turned-down oil-lamps. He tiptoed past an open door and glanced in. An old lady was nodding over a book, by another dying fire. Anne felt a wave of great affection sweep over the Old Feller. Nanny. Or governess.

The Old Feller was halfway downstairs when another door banged, and urgent voices drifted down. The Old Feller dived for a cupboard. It was full of boots, and smelt strongly of dubbin.

Through the cupboard door, left open a crack, Anne watched a man and woman hurry past. The man wore a greatcoat with huge flaps over the shoulders. He had a dark urgent face, like a hawk. The woman was beautiful, but pale and agitated. Another wave of affection swept over the Old Feller. Mother and Father, Anne presumed.

The man said, 'It *is* my concern. It could be the *Victoria*. She's four days overdue. That fool Simpson under-insured her at Lloyd's. If it is the *Victoria* then we're halfway to ruin.'

The front door banged shut behind them. The Old Feller waited a few minutes, then followed.

He ran down ten steps into a fine Georgian square. No street-lights, only a guttering lamp over the door of every house. And the moon was up. The clouds that might have covered it had been torn to rags by the wind. The wind threw the Old Feller against a brick wall as he turned the corner.

He was not alone. Everywhere, people hurrying towards the sea. Men struggling to hold their tall

178

hats; women with shawls pulled round their faces. Ragged boys and girls ran, shrieking with excitement. Their feet were bare, though the air was bitter cold.

How strong the wind was! The people passed, leaving the Old Feller struggling behind. It was a very long way; but at last he turned in to a broad street lined with white cottages; red pantiled roofs. The street seemed familiar, and yet unfamiliar.

Then Anne saw a shape she knew. Garmouth Priory, at the far end, outlined by the moon. She was in Front Street. Front Street paved with cobbles from end to end. And carriages coming towards her up Front street. Carriage-lamps flickering to death in the wind. Iron tyres rumbling on the cobbles. Horses' hooves sparking, as they struggled against the gale that threw the light wooden carriages into their hind-quarters. Coachmen shouting soothing words, and the horses' eyes rolling white.

Why were they driving away from the sea? Why were the other people coming back in crowds? The Old Feller dodged in a doorway to avoid being seen.

Women were weeping. 'Oh, those poor souls.'

'Not a chance,' said a man. 'Never a chance. Did you see the lifeboat? Couldn't make a yard against the gale. It was all they could do to save themselves. It should never have been launched.'

'You have to try,' said another. 'You have to do what you can.'

'It'll be splinters by now; splinters and fish-food. Not a whole corpse ashore.'

'Was it the *Victoria*?'

'Na. It was the *Hoplite*.'

179

'There'll be widows. More work for the Guardians.'

The crowd passed and thinned. The Old Feller ducked out into the wind again. But a hand fell on his shoulder.

'Boy! Boy, what are you doing here?'

In a second, the Old Feller was the centre of a large family group, all bending over him. The speaker, the father, was a grey-haired clergyman.

'Going to see the wreck,' stammered the Old Feller.

'Too late. Nothing left to see. For Christian folk.' Everyone fell silent. Everyone knew who would remain, searching for rings on drowned fingers.

'Come, boy, we will take you home.' The old clergyman turned to where his rather shabby carriage waited, horse bracing its legs and leaning back into the wind. He let go of the Old Feller to help his wife and daughters aboard.

The Old Feller took to his heels, down a dark alleyway between two cottages.

The Old Feller ran down the mud track from Front Street. The track was slippery. He fell twice, but he hardly noticed, he was so excited. Anne could see the bay on her left, but there was no yacht club; just a rank of black fishing-boats, pulled well back from the high-tide mark, and some black huts.

The track led up on to Watch House Cliff; but there was no Watch House; just gorse-bushes that tossed and flogged wildly in the gale.

Eastwards, under the ragged moon, the sea crawled towards the shore like a mass of serried roofs, black and grey. Roofs steep-pitched and thirty feet high.

180

Pushing into a Gar estuary without benefit of piers; a Gar estuary that only funnelled them and made them higher, wilder. So that wave mounted wave like mating stallions; crossing each other, colliding in boiling chaos from which new waves leapt in new directions to collide again. But always their force grew more, not less.

And then Anne saw the Middens of a hundred years ago. Middens clutching the boiling Gar like a spread hand of six fingers. Spray drifted at the fingertips, but they were not the killing-point. The killing-point was the gullies between the fingers, where the waves rushed in ascending fury, higher, higher, higher, to burst with a report like a gun where the black fingers met.

At that report, the water leapt like a shell from a gun, curving, thinning, in a great trajectory that reached as far as the clifftop.

The first time, the Old Feller flinched. But he needn't have bothered. By the time the water reached his face it was no heavier than fine rain.

The black hand of the Middens buried itself in turmoil, again and again. But never for long. Each time it rose from the shambles of cross-currents, glistening like patent-leather in the moonlight. Then going dull; then burying itself again under the waves, reaching for the hulls of ships as though it were a living thing.

Boom, boom, boom went the gullies in strict order, starting from the river's mouth. *Boom, boom, boom, boom, boom*, like a ship firing a salvo. The second gully was loudest, the fifth softest, being smaller and nearer land. Their rhythm seemed to hypnotize the

181

Old Feller; their flights of foam thrown like disintegrating birds. The salt on his face made him lick his lips time and again.

Then he noticed the men on the Middens.

There were five, standing outlined against the fluorescence of the breakers, like black birds. They must be soaked to the skin. Every so often they vanished completely in the spray.

The Old Feller knew they were wreckers, evil men. Every so often they would pick something up, shouting to each other in harsh indecipherable voices. Then they would throw the thing back into the waves. Once the Old Feller thought, with a gulp of disgust, that they threw back a human arm. But it was too far off to see properly. Trembling all over, he found a low place in the cliff, and slithered down.

When he looked again, from his hiding-place among the higher, drier rocks, there was a sixth figure, staggering along the wave's edge towards the others. A giant figure, carrying something under one arm, and waving the other triumphantly.

The five wreckers gave back from the sea's edge, to form a semi-circle that blocked the giant's way to dry land.

Too late, he noticed. Stopped shouting and waving. Stopped walking and fell into a wary crouch. He did not let go of the object under his left arm, but transferred it to his right fist.

'Let me through, Johnson. It's me, Hague, home from Australia. Don't try your thieving tricks on me. I know you all. Johnson, Beavers, Renshaw, Hawke, Dobie.'

Anne shuddered. The five names from the desecrated graves.

But now the wreckers were shouting back. 'Aye, and we know you, Hague. Australia, eh? There's gold in Australia. What you got in that ditty-box, Hague?'

'Army papers. And *Major* Hague to you. Major Hague of the Fifty-fifth.'

'Let's see your papers, *Major* Hague.'

'I'll see you in hell, first.'

'Show us the *papers*, or it's you will be in hell.'

Next second, Hague made his run. Across the rocks he came, straight for where the Old Feller was hiding. And in spite of the gale, and the slippery rocks and the heavy ditty-box, he came fast.

The wreckers darted in, like dogs at a bear. Hague raised the ditty-box aloft, and smashed it down on the first man's head. The man fell like a piece of wreckage, and the others drew back.

Hague paused for breath. Anne could see his great chest heaving, under the red tunic. 'Aye, there's Beavers in hell for a start. Who's next?' Hague ran again.

Again the wreckers closed, things glittering in their hands. Again the terrible ditty-box rose and fell, and a man fell with it. But now something was terribly wrong with Hague. He still ran, but his arms and legs weren't working properly; he ran sideways, like a crab, and there was a dark stain spreading down his sodden tunic. His mouth was open in one long rushing scream of air.

Nearer and nearer he ran, till he towered over the Old Feller's hiding place, higher than the sky. Then he crashed in ruin, across the very rock behind which the Old Feller was hiding. His face, streaked with wet blond hair, was only a yard from the Old Feller's.

His blue eyes opened, dazed. He saw the Old Feller for the first time. His great hand reached out.

'Help me! *Help* me!'

A shout came from further off. 'He's down lads. He can't hurt you now. C'mon, finish him.'

The Old Feller drew back from the clutching hand, the staring beseeching face, into the crevices of a dry gully; into the dark.

There was an unbearable noise from Hague. Then silence.

'That's it, then,' said a man, satisfied.

'He's done for Beavers. And Dobie.'

'More shares for us.'

'Where's that ditty-box?'

'Can't get his hand loose from it.'

'It's a death-grip. Ye won't brek that.'

'Aah'll brek it. Gies yer big knife.'

There was a deep grating noise and a crack. Then only silence and darkness.

'Poor little sod,' said Timmo. 'All that guilt, all those years.'

'You mean he never told anybody? You mean he lived alone with it, all his life?' said Pat.

'Probably. Hague's memorial tablet says "drowned at sea" not "foully murdered".'

'But *why*?'

'Who knows, with a ten-year-old? Maybe when he wakened up in the morning, he hoped it was just a bad dream. Then the body never turned up, and nobody asked him questions. And he spent a lifetime paying for it. Rescue at sea. It must have been horrible for him when people began piling shipwreck relics into his Watch House. Stuff that could turn up any time, from anywhere. The skull; and then the figurehead.'

'*Which* figurehead?' asked Anne.

Timmo pointed to the huge rotting warrior in the garden. 'The one they never brought into the Watch House. Don't you know what a hoplite was? A Greek soldier.'

19

There was a yellow car parked, when they got outside. It should have warned Anne, but it didn't. Her mind was too full of what had just happened.

There was a woman standing by the cottage gate. A thin elegant woman with a headscarf round her hair, tied behind in the fashionable way. A woman with a discontented mouth and a nervous hand at her throat. A born loser. Anne felt a momentary pity. Till she saw that it was Mother.

'What do *you* want?' said Anne. She didn't mean to be rude or cruel. It was just that she couldn't get her mind out of the other business fast enough.

'I'm taking you back to London,' said Mother.

Anne felt Timmo and Pat freeze, one on each side of her. They stared at Mother in open horror. Anne knew she was staring at Mother in open horror, too.

'Don't stand there dreaming,' said Mother. 'It's a long drive.'

'These are my friends. Timothy Jones and Pat Pierson.'

Timmo and Pat stayed silent too long. Then said 'Hallo' in a rush, together.

'This is my mother.'

'Hallo,' said Mother, without interest, already turning into the cottage gate. As if Timmo and Pat were no more than woodlice on the cottage gate or something.

'We'll hang around,' said Timmo quietly. He and Pat drifted off to stare at the river, standing very close together.

Anne went into the cottage, pushing roughly at the oilskins and reefer-jackets as she passed.

Prudie was rushing round between living room and kitchen like a wild thing, arms full of Anne's half-dried washing. 'You'll have to air these things as soon as you get home, Miss Fiona. They're not fit for packing really . . . a polythene bag . . . Arthur, go and fetch me a polythene bag. Then there's her bicycle that she bought. She's hardly used it . . . are you sure you can't take it with you? It seems such a waste. And there's her Wellingtons by the back door. Arthur, go and get Miss Anne's Wellingtons . . .'

Prudie was pale, chewing at her lower lip. She wouldn't look at Anne at all. She kept dropping things and picking them up again.

Arthur sat in his rocking chair, doing nothing but glaring at Mother.

Anne stood watching them all. Prudie battling with tears. Arthur sitting on his bottled-up rage. Timmo and Pat, clearly in view through the window, disconsolate on the cliff-edge. Everyone thrown in confusion to suit Mother's whim. Mother having it all her own way *again*.

'Come on, Anne. Don't stand there gawping.'

'I'm not coming with you.'

Prudie froze in mid-stride, a pair of Anne's blue pants held aloft. There was a great silence. It seemed to Anne that even Timmo and Pat heard that silence. They turned and looked at the house.

'I *beg* your pardon?' said Mother icily.

'I'm not coming with you. I'm going to stay here till Daddy comes for me.'

'You little fool. The court gave you to *me*.' Mother clutched at Anne's wrist.

'Let *go* of me!' shouted Anne desperately trying to control an urge to attack Mother physically. Now everything was bubbling out, it was hard.

But she must keep cool.

She must win over Prudie, who was looking shocked to death.

'Let me *go*!'

'Then stop behaving ridiculously.'

'I am *not* behaving ridiculously. Let me *go*!' Anne gave a heave and broke free. She'd never before realized that she was physically stronger than Mother. Never even realized till now that she was taller than Mother.

Mother licked her lips and tried a tolerant smile. 'Come on, Anne. I know this must be a shock to you. I should have written, but I've been so busy. I know it means leaving all the friends you've made. But life's like that. You can come back for a holiday next year. Can't she, Prudie?'

Prudie nodded dumbly, tears in her eyes.

'I'm not coming for a holiday next summer, because I'm not leaving *now*.'

'You have no choice,' said Mother. 'I have Care and Custody.'

'You haven't. When you went back to live with Daddy the last time, the Care and Custody order

188

lapsed. You'll have to go to court all over again. And do you know who the judge will listen to? Me. *Me*! The court will consult the child's wishes and preferences at all times. I was too little to be asked the last time. But I'm not too little now.'

'Who told you this rubbish?'

'Mr McGill.'

Anne felt Prudie and Arthur start, at the mention of the name.

'And who is Mr McGill?' asked Mother scornfully.

'*My* solicitor.'

Mother laughed. 'A small-town hack, touting for business. He's picked a loser in you. You've got no money.'

'Watch how you mention Mr McGill in my house, Missus.' Arthur's voice was low but very unfriendly. Prudie was bristling too. Mother realized for the first time that she was on a hostile shore. She attempted a light laugh, which didn't work very well.

'I'm sure I didn't mean to insult your friend, Arthur. But it stands to reason I should look after Anne. I *am* her mother and it's my house she should be in.'

Anne watched Mother. Mother seemed even more desperate than the situation warranted. Why? Had it all gone wrong with Monty? Had she failed to find a job? But having Anne wouldn't solve either of those situations. What was Mother up to?

Daddy. Supposing things weren't going so badly for Daddy after all? And Mother had heard? She had friends who would know that kind of thing. Perhaps Mother was angling for a reconciliation, and wanting Anne as bait. And Daddy would fall for it. Soft, silly Daddy.

It was Daddy's softness that made Anne cruel now.

'I don't want to live with you. I can't stand having that *man* around the place all the time.'

Mother gasped softly at such treachery. Arthur and Prudie's faces had set like flint, at the mention of a *man*.

'*What* man?' said Mother, through another failed laugh. 'You mean Uncle Monty? He's just a friend, you silly goose. He's just helping me settle in, that's all . . .'

'By spending all night in your bedroom while Daddy's away?' Anne had to force herself to say it; but she said it.

'How can you make up such nonsense about Uncle Monty?' asked Mother, in her surely-to-goodness voice.

'He can't keep his hands off *me* either. He's always trying to touch me, when you're not watching. And give me wet open-mouth kisses.' It was true. So why was it so terrible to say it?

The atmosphere of disapproval in the room was now so thick you could have cut it with a knife.

'I don't have to stand here and be talked to like this,' said Mother. 'Not by my own daughter.' She sounded dazed.

'Is all this true, Miss Fiona?' asked Prudie. Suddenly she looked stern, as she used to years ago; on the few occasions Anne had been smacked for naughtiness.

'Is *what* true?' asked Mother. She obviously couldn't believe it was happening.

'About the *man*.' Sixty years of Non-conformist

chapel were in Prudie's voice. They made her sound like the Day of Judgement.

'What's that got to do with you?' said Mother. 'It's no business of yours how I lead my life.'

'This bairn is my business.'

'Don't be ridiculous. I brought her for a holiday and now I'm taking her back.'

'Not before I've spoken to the Welfare,' said Prudie. 'It's over my head, this. But that bairn does not leave this house till I've spoken to the Welfare. Where's my reading-glasses, Arthur?'

Arthur moved for the first time, and moved quickly. Prudie put on her gold-rimmed spectacles, and picked up the telephone directory from the bookcase, where it lay between the Bible and the *Universal Home Doctor*. She began to run her licked finger down the pages.

'It's called Social Services now,' said Arthur with helpful malice. 'Aah has to ring them sometimes for shipwrecked fellers. Letting their wives know an' all ... specially foreign fellers. Garmouth 42298.' Prudie picked up the phone in the hall.

'I don't have to stand for this!' shrieked Mother. 'I'll not stand here and let bloody interfering do-gooders pry into my affairs ...'

'The front door's open, hinny,' said Arthur.

Mother made an indescribable noise compounded of rage and disgust, and was gone. They watched the yellow car streak up the hill to Garmouth.

'Eeeh,' said Prudie. 'Aah feel quite faint.' She sat down suddenly in Arthur's rocking-chair. Anne and Arthur fussed towards her, but she pushed them away. 'Aah'll be all right in a minute, when Aah've got me breath. Make us a cup o' tea, will ye, Anne? And Arthur, ring up Mr McGill and ask him to call. And,' she gave Anne a very severe look, 'Aah think Aah better write to yer Da tonight.'

Anne filled the kettle with shaking hands. She realized Timmo and Pat had their noses to the kitchen window, and gave a shaky thumbs-up.

'Have you won?' asked Timmo through the window. 'God, you look *awful*. I'd hate to see you when you lose.'

'If that's Master Timothy,' said Prudie, eyes still shut, 'tell him there's a door to this house.'

Timmo and Pat stayed for what Prudie called 'a scratch tea'; the delicious leftovers of three days. Everyone ate like pigs out of sheer relief. Arthur attempted to unfasten the top button of his trousers, and was firmly made to rebutton it by Prudie.

Afterwards, they went and sat on the cliffs, in the cool of the day.

'How d'you feel' asked Pat, 'now it's over?'

'Dazed,' said Anne. 'I only hope Daddy will *want* me, after this. But most of all I feel *empty*. Mummy's made our lives a misery for so long. She seemed so big and powerful. She filled the whole world. Everything depended upon what Mummy thought and said. She once cancelled a whole trip to France just like *that*. I always felt so helpless . . .

'And now she's just, well, another middle-aged woman driving back to her flat in London . . . Her power's sort of gone. Now I can't even see where she got it from.'

'That's easy enough,' said Timmo. '*You* gave it to

her; and your father gave it to her. The more you gave in to her, the bigger and more awful she got . . . sorry, it's your family. I shouldn't be talking like this . . .'

'I don't mind. It's true enough what you say. Daddy gave her all that power like . . . like . . .'

'Like the Old Feller gave Hague his power.'

The two girls gaped at Timmo. He shrugged.

'Well . . . can a ghost *be* a ghost when there's no one to frighten? No more than Robinson Crusoe could be a bully before Man Friday turned up. It sounds a horrible thing to say, but don't ghosts, like people, feed on other people? What would Hitler have been if everyone had just laughed at him? An unemployed disgruntled house-painter.'

'So?'

'Maybe Hague got so big *feeding* on the Old Feller's terror. Just as the Old Feller has got sort of . . . bigger and noisier because you listened to him, Anne. I mean, before you came, the old men of the Brigade just treated the Old Feller as a sort of joke. So he didn't do much, just nagged in little ways. Footsteps, knocking things over. But you came, and you were alone and lonely, and soft-hearted . . . and *cared*.'

'You mean the Old Feller's feeding on *me*?'

'Yes, if you like. Not nastily. But he's not doing you much *good*, is he? You've lost half a stone in weight. You were desperate . . .'

'I'm not desperate any more!'

'All the same, the sooner the whole thing is finished with, the better.'

'But how?'

'I'll have to think,' said Timmo.

193

20

'C'mon,' said Timmo. 'We're leaving early. You need some beauty sleep, my girl.'

'But *why*? I'm next with Ginger at table tennis!'

'Home,' said Timmo firmly. Pat had moved up beside him. She was wearing a cheap flashy crucifix, and was twisting her fingers round it.

'But it's only nine o'clock,' protested Anne.

'We've got things to do. But we'll see you home first.'

Anne glanced out of the youth club window. It was growing dark. It was an offer she didn't want to refuse.

As they left, Timmo dropped behind. When he caught them up again, he was carrying something long wrapped in sacking. He carried it on the side of him away from Anne. Pat was between them, and Anne, peer as she might, couldn't make out what it was.

'What's that?'

'Want some chips?' said Timmo enticingly.

'No, I don't want some chips. I want to know what you're carrying.'

'My own business.' They walked along in a semi-huff. Timmo began singing silly words to *La Donna é Mobile*. Singing silly words to classical tunes by people like Beethoven and Verdi was the thing Timmo did that most annoyed Anne. She knew he was trying to annoy her now.

Then he let the long thing in sacking droop, so it just touched the pavement. There was a tiny clink that could only mean garden-spade.

'It's a spade!'

'Give the lady the sixty-four thousand dollar prize,' said Timmo sarcastically. 'So I'm carrying a spade. Is there a law in English legislature that says I may not carry my own spade? Or rather my revered father's spade?'

'What's it for?' They turned the corner by the Memorial Clock, and began walking down the bank to the pier.

'Not saying,' said Timmo. She had never known him so irritating.

'What's it *for*?'

So it went on, until Pat said, in a burst of irritation, 'Oh, for Heaven's sake, you two. Stop it. I feel like a United Nations buffer-zone. Tell her, Timmo.'

'Gardening,' said Timmo. 'I've gone Friends of the Earth at last. I have felt it creeping up on me for some days, like a hideous disease. There is no cure. I must face it with my usual well-known courage.'

'Cow manure!' said Pat. 'Death, where is thy sting?' It should have been funny, but the laugh came out wrong. And why did she keep on twisting that crucifix? She'd have it snapped off its chain in a minute.

When they reached the hawthorn hedge that bordered the Watch House garden, Timmo said, 'Hang on a bit. Nature calls.'

'You can go at Prudie's . . .'

But Timmo was away, through a gap in the hedge, leaving Pat holding the spade.

'I hope this Friends of the Earth thing doesn't go on too long. I do really *hate* the smell of manure . . .' But she was just talking for talking's sake. Anne suddenly pushed her aside, and made for the gap in the hedge.

There was the big black telegraph pole in the middle of the Watch House garden. There was the Watch House itself, glimmering faintly in the moonlight. For a horrid second, she thought she saw a pale figure standing by the Watch House door. But it was only the figurehead from the *Hoplite*.

Then she realized the sash-window of the billiard-room was wide open. As she watched, a dark figure jumped out over the sill.

'It's all right. It's only Timmo. He left the window open deliberately.'

'What's he *doing*?'

'Oh, nothing much.'

The dark figure looked left and right, and began sidling carefully down the lawn. He was carrying something in his hand; something in a plastic carrier-bag.

'What's he got?' Anne started to say. But her breath caught in her throat.

'The skull. He says it's time for a painless extraction. You won't feel a thing.'

'Why?'

Pat giggled; not a very happy giggle. 'We're planting it for good, where it belongs – in the Priory graveyard.'

'Why didn't you *tell* me?'

'Timmo said it was better if you weren't *involved*. Better safe than sorry, he said.'

There was a movement by the Watch House door again. Anne's heart was in her mouth. Suppose Arthur . . . but it was only the figurehead from the *Hoplite* again. Silly.

And then she saw it *was* moving; rocking on its base. All six feet of it. As if something was straining to lift it. Oh, God, it was just the moonlight working on her imagination. She must get a grip on herself.

Then it lifted right out of the ground. She could hear grass-roots tearing from the earth as it came. Then it made straight for Timmo. Jerkily, as if something was carrying it. Except the lumps of rotten wood breaking off the bottom made a movement like legs, and left a trail of fragments, like footsteps on the turf.

'Oh my God!' moaned Pat between her teeth.

Silently it gained on Timmo. Silent, but for the whisper of falling fragments. He sensed something was behind him, turned, stood paralysed by the incredible sight. It reared high above him, to smash him to a pulp. As in a nightmare, Anne struggled to find her voice.

'Timmo!'

Just in time he moved; swerved behind the telegraph pole on the lawn. The great figurehead with its grey helmet, cracked grey shield and dark blind eyes crashed into the pole and burst into a thousand rotting fragments. The telegraph pole rocked but did not fall.

Timmo ran up to them. 'Quick, this way. Under

cover.' A light had gone on in Brigade Cottage. Prudie's bedroom.

They plunged through a gap in a mass of brambles, and dropped into a shallow trench with concrete sides. Timmo laughed shakily.

'I knew he *threw* things, but . . . Anyway, that'll have used up his kinetic energy for a bit. Won't it, old chap?' He gave the plastic carrier-bag a friendly joggle. It was a bag from Tesco Supermarket.

Brigade Cottage door opened, casting a swathe of light across the Watch House grass. Arthur walked down in dressing-gown and slippers. Prudie lingered nervously in the doorway, shouting instructions about being careful.

'It's the figurehead,' shouted Arthur back. 'Smashed to bits. Bloody vandals. Ring for the Poliss, Prudie. They're not getting away with this.'

'Come on,' whispered Timmo. 'There'll be a Panda-car along in a minute.'

Anne hesitated. She had a wild desire to run out to Arthur; to run out to the real world of Pandas and vandals and righteous indignation.

'Come *on*,' whispered Timmo. 'We're doing this for *you*.' He pulled a hand-lantern from the pocket of his anorak. Just for a second, he got the switch wrong, and the dome on top lit up. Red, darkness, red, darkness, danger. Then he got the white beam to work, and pointed along the shallow trench. Under the roof of briars, along the floor or long dead grass, ran a rusty railway line.

'It's the old wagon-way for fetching the stones when the pier was being built. Leads straight to the foot of the Priory cliff. Good, eh? I spent all the morning reconnoitring it.'

'But what's the point of all this?'

'You know what old da Souza told you about relics? Well, I reckon he was right. Sound man, in his own pathetically narrow field, da Souza. The only reason old Hague had any power in the Watch House is that his skull was there. Give it a decent Christian burial in holy ground, and what gripe's he got left? Leave him to Heaven . . .'

'But you aren't a Christian!'

'No, but Pat is, and she's brought her prayer-book to prove it. Handy thing to have around, a Christian. They come in useful on occasion.'

'But you can't prove any of this.'

'I don't have to. Hague just has. You don't think he threw the remains of the *Hoplite* at me for laughs, do you? He's not just narked – he's really worried. He knows the game's up – *if* we can get the skull decently buried in the graveyard.'

'If . . . ?'

'He's not just going to stand by and let us. Are you, old chap?' He gave the Tesco carrier-bag another friendly joggle. 'Yes, we can expect dirty tricks all the way to the graveyard.'

As they passed under the wooden bridge that carried the main road across the trench, a police car rumbled overhead with siren going and flashing blue lights. Anne felt she would go crazy, split between two worlds.

'C'mon,' said Timmo, 'before we have them after us as well.'

It was a nightmare journey. A worrying little

sporadic wind had got up, turning the long grass and gorse-bushes of the place into an orchestra of inexplicable noise that could be hiding other noises. The very trench itself seemed hostile. Briars reached down from the roof and snagged their clothes; and it needed someone to hold the torch close before you could disentangle. The old railway line lay in the long dead grass, in wait for unwary feet. There were loose stones in the grass, too, with sharp edges, that turned under your ankle. The lantern-light seemed to shatter into a thousand twisting shapes, with pitch blackness beyond. There was a temptation to break out of the black-and-yellow web of their slow lamplit progress. Anywhere . . . until they suddenly found themselves on the cliff-edge, where no cliff-edge ought to be. Or was.

'Slow and steady,' said Timmo. 'Panic is Hague's stock-in-trade. I think it's what he *lives* on.'

The trench came to an end at last, and they were climbing the open grassy bank to the Priory. Below and far away, Front Street seemed another world; a cool, calm miniature world of lighted pubs and double-decker buses.

Then something cold, damp and all-enveloping wrapped itself round Anne's face. She screamed and dropped the lantern, trying to claw it off.

Next second, the cold wet thing was snatched away. 'Polythene bag,' said Timmo grimly. 'He's getting his strength back. Well, that's it with the lantern. Bulb's gone. Lucky I've got another torch. Two more, actually. But don't make a habit of dropping them, Anne, will you? It's a bit hard on the old pocket-money.'

They were in the graveyard now. Gravestones swam into the light of the torch: THE BURIAL PLACE OF JOHN STEELE, MASTER AND MARINER OF CULLERCOATS MARY HIS WIFE DIED NOV 2ND 1763 ALICE HIS DAUGHTER DIED DEC 15TH 1793 AGED 43.

'We'll keep clear of the Priory ruins,' said Timmo. 'There could be some loose stones up top he could fetch down on us.' He began stamping the turf. 'I'm looking for good deep soil. This whole place is a mass of buried stones. This sounds likely. Hold the torch steady.'

He cut a turf out, and dug quickly, but reached stone after only a foot.

'Damn, I'll try again.' But twice more he reached stone quickly. Pat's teeth were starting to chatter, though she stoutly maintained it was just the cold.

'Oh, this'll have to do.' He tipped up the Tesco bag. The dome of the skull glinted, and vanished into the black hole. 'Got your prayer-book, Pat?'

Pat fumbled in her anorak. 'Hold the torch here, Anne, will you?' Her hands were shaking; she had a lot of trouble finding the place. And the printing was so small in the torchlight. 'Oh, where shall I start? There's so much of it.'

'Just start,' said Timmo grimly.

The bulb of the torch flickered and went out. Timmo flicked the second torch on, straight away. But he could feel the panic gathering in the girls.

'OK. We'll scrub the service.' He stamped the earth down on top of the skull, and gave it three good whacks with a spade. 'Ashes to ashes and dust to dust. We commit this body to the earth. We'll come back and say a proper service in the morning.'

They ran away, as fast as the dark would let them.

21

Next morning, the sun was shining. The sea was calm, and Anne ate the biggest breakfast she had ever eaten. Prudie even said she had a crop for all corn, which was the Olympic gold as far as eating was concerned.

After breakfast, she did not feel like moving. She cheekily pinched Arthur's morning paper off his chair and began digesting the details of such happy things as burnt-out hot-dog stalls at pop-festivals.

Arthur had no use for his paper this morning. She could hear him coming and going with great briskness; nagging Prudie for dusters and Windowlene. Every so often they would start a fresh tirade against the vandals; but there was an excitement in Arthur's voice that had nothing to do with vandalism.

'There! What do you think of that, Miss Anne?'

She looked up from *Runaway Vicar Cited in Divorce Case*. Arthur was holding aloft a picture-frame. Inside, instead of a picture, there was a layer of black velvet, covered with examples of Arthur's fancy-knots, in shiny white string.

'Oh, Arthur, that's lovely!'

'Aah'm going to hang it in the billiard-room. Aah must just get a bit of twine for the back. Will you go and open up the Watch House for me, Miss Anne?'

She went willingly. As she came through the cottage

gate, she looked up towards Front Street. A yellow anorak and a blue one were just descending the bank. They waved. Anne waved back. The burial party was on its way, prayer-book and all. Nothing could stop them now.

She stepped up to the Watch House door, keys in hand. There was something on the step . . .

How she stopped herself from screaming she would never know. It was the skull. One of the cheek-bones was chipped; its eye-sockets were full of soil. But it was the skull all right.

Behind her, far off as in a dream, she could hear Arthur bickering with Prudie. He would be here in a minute.

He must not see the skull in that condition. She must get it back in the glass case.

She shut her eyes and picked it up. She could tell from its gnawed saliva-ish feel that it was the dog from the graveyard that had brought it back.

'Steady,' said Timmo. 'Steady, for Pete's sake. Hold both my hands and try and stop shaking.'

'Shall I get Prudie?' asked Pat.

'*No!*' that was one thing of which Anne was *quite* certain.

'What happened?'

'That dog brought it back. I had to pick it up, and . . . I had to clean it. I couldn't risk Arthur seeing it like that. It was horrible. It felt like being its . . . body-servant.'

'The bastard. The bloody bastard.' Timmo wasn't scared at all. He sounded so angry that his anger was scaring. 'Oh, knowing that dog . . . I forgot about

204

that dog . . . it would probably have dug it up anyway. But what possessed it to bring the bloody thing back here?'

'That's a good question,' said Pat. 'What *possessed* it?' She shuddered nearly as badly as Anne.

'This time,' said Timmo, 'I'm going to deal with it and deal with it good. Six feet down, and be damned to the graveyard-keeper. I only wish I could bury all its other bones as well, for good measure. But they'll be scattered all over the Middens.'

'I don't think so,' said Anne faintly.

'What you mean?'

'Well, something funny happened to me when I first came here. Out on the Middens. I had a kind of waking nightmare that I was drowning. Arthur had to save me. I think it might have been . . . him.'

'Where?' said Timmo.

'It started on the furthest point of the Middens,' said Anne. 'Where the basket is, set up on a post.'

Timmo looked out of the window. 'Tide's right down. Well, there's no time like the present. Where does Arthur keep his spade?'

'What'll you tell him?'

'Oh, haven't you heard? I've taken up fishing. The Black Middens's a lovely place for digging up lug-worms.'

Anne sat on the Middens, tense as a cat. The whole world conspired to reassure her. Small white clouds floated prettily; the breeze was a gentle warm hand; the Gar – from this low down anyway – sparkled as blue as the Mediterranean. There were even two jolly young men in a red-sailed dinghy who considered her

of interest, and waved and shouted jovial incompre-
hensibilities at the end of every tack. College types,
from the heraldic devices on their T-shirts; nice.

But it didn't make a ha'porth of difference. She sat
hunched up like a shrivelled crab and responded to
none of it.

It was all being too easy. Timmo had charmed a
spade and a washing-up bowl and an old fish-bag out
of Arthur. All Arthur had said was that they had a
nice day for it. Then she had taken Timmo out to the
basket-on-the-post. The rocks around the post, for a
distance of twenty yards, revealed only one place
where bones might lie. An oblong pot-hole much the
size of a coffin, though more irregular. All the other
fissures were inch-wide cracks that wouldn't conceal
a shrimp.

Somehow, the good luck only made Anne more
miserable. Timmo had turned to her and said, 'You
sit back a bit, Anne, and keep a look-out. There's any
amount of dirty tricks . . . and you know *him* best.
Keep us covered.'

But what dirty tricks could there be? The tide was
right out. The waves in the river all of three inches
high. There was hardly enough wind to keep that
sailing-dinghy moving. On the shore, a bright yellow
bread-van had just pulled up to Brigade Cottage . . .

For half an hour, Timmo had dug steadily, but in
vain. Pat kept carrying bowls of black sludge to the
water's edge, and tipped and washed them slowly
into the river. They made a spreading black stain
on the water that flowed past Anne, about ten yards
out. It was strange how cool Pat looked, how professional. It was obvious that she and Timmo had

done some archaeological digging at some time. Another of Timmo's fleeting obsessions, no doubt. But it was more than that. Pat drew a great steadiness from being Timmo's helper. Perhaps they'd get married in course of time. She couldn't imagine them ever being apart for long. But perhaps Timmo didn't believe in marriage . . . Anne caught herself hoping they would find no bones. *Why* did she hope they would find no bones? Didn't she want this thing cleared up?

Anyway, her hopes were soon dashed. There was a whoop from Timmo, and she looked up to see Pat brandishing a long brown object.

'Right femur . . . a big one.' Anne stayed where she was. She didn't want to see it. It made her feel worse.

After that, shouts about vertebrae and scapula, tibia and fibula became monotonous. The trench was not deep, apparently. Hague had lain for over a century, covered by only a foot or so of ooze. If it was Hague . . .

But the distant sounds of triumph only made Anne feel more isolated. Why was she such a coward? She was withdrawing further and further away from them; and from the young men in the dinghy; and from Arthur, distantly busy on the cliff-top. Everything was like something on television; or something in an old, brown faded picture . . .

'Hey, wake up! We're finished. We've got most of him; all of him there is.'

She looked up with a jump. Timmo and Pat, mud-stained but grinning. Pat holding the shovel and the bowl; Timmo the fish-bag. The yellow straw bag was stained grey and wet, halfway up its sides. It dripped

207

grey water. It didn't look very full or very heavy. How little comprised a man. But then the skull wasn't there.

'C'mon, let's get cracking. I'll nick the skull as we pass. Arthur's gone in for his cuppa.'

They made their way slowly to shore. The tide had gained six inches, but that was nothing. The sky had lost its little white clouds. It was now just blue. Yet Anne felt as if everything and everyone in the world was watching; as they might watch a funeral procession with black cars. She kept glancing round, to the point of stupidity. Left, right, up, down, behind. Nothing.

Nothing except the Gallower, who had left his grazing, and was peering cautiously over the edge of the cliff.

Her legs were reluctant. She had to keep on telling them to walk. She lagged further and further behind. Timmo and Pat's cheerful chatter faded. Which was good. It wasn't right to chatter, where there was so much danger.

The Gallower *was* being nosy. He was following Pat and Timmo, along the cliff-top, peering over at intervals. What was he up to? Pushing against that fencing. He'd have it over in a minute. *And* that notice-board! It wasn't very strong fencing or a well-made notice-board. Typical Arthur.

And then she remembered what the other side of the notice-board said.

DANGER – CLIFF-FALLS.

She saw it all in a flash. The poor wire fence that the Gallower was breasting through. The great pinnacles of dry soil immediately below. The cracks in

208

the cliff. As she watched, the fence-posts sagged, and a little trickle of dry soil plunged down the cliff, only to be caught in a crevice before it could reach the path in front of Pat and Timmo.

Anne's legs seized up. She tried to shout a warning, but only a funny little sighing burp came out of her mouth. The muscles of her throat had tightened into an iron band.

She filled her lungs for a great convulsive effort, as she saw the Gallower take another step forward, and the first pinnacle of soil move sideways.

'Timmo!'

They stopped, directly under the pinnacles. They turned round to wait for her, with faintly questioning looks on their faces; faint frowns of impatience. It was all so microscopically detailed, like the best kind of photographs . . .

Then her knees gave way, and she fell.

Timmo dropped the fish-bag. Pat dropped the shovel, and they began to run back towards her. As the whole cliff-face above them lifted out into space, with the Gallower, straddle-legged, on top.

Then there was just Timmo and Pat running, against the backdrop of billowing clouds of brown dust like an explosion. The rushing rumble of sound came quite separately, afterwards. She was always sure of that, ever after. The sound came quite separately.

They plunged down beside her, arms over their heads in a shower of soil and pebbles. *Rumble, whoof, rumble, whoof.* Section after section of the cliff fell. Dust, dust, dust.

Then silence.

'Oh, my God, I can't see,' wailed Pat.

They staggered to their feet, Pat's eyes blinking rapidly, tears cutting watercourses in the caked dust of her cheeks; Timmo swearing in a continuous monotone, brushing the earth out of his hair.

The dust-cloud was settling, drifting away like a yellow ghost out into the river.

The rocks had vanished. The whole shape of the cliff had changed. It was no longer vertical, but a forty-five degree slope. At the bottom of the slope lay the Gallower, so covered with dust he looked like a clay-model of a horse. They walked over to him. There was a fine layer of dust over the cunning bright little eye they could see. The eye did not blink the dust away. Anne tried to raise his head; but it came up with a funny easy motion that told her that his neck was broken.

'He's dead.'

A rush of soil and stones from above made them jump back hastily. But it was only Arthur, treading down the shallow slope in great fifteen-foot steps.

Arthur looked at the Gallower. Then he looked at Anne.

'Aah should have made that fence stronger. Only he always kept clear of the edge. Aah never thought.'

'I'm sorry,' said Anne, tears running down her cheeks that were not caused by the dust.

'He was a crafty old sod,' said Arthur. 'Ye ought to've seen him pinching apples off the greengrocer's cart.'

'Is there anything we can do?'

'No, Miss Anne. Even the men from the knacker's yard wouldn't want him now – too much bother getting him up the cliff to be worth their while. No, the next two tides will tek' him out to sea. I'd rather have that for him than the knacker's yard. That's the way they buried the old Viking chiefs, you know. Out to sea. He would have liked that.'

Anne stared helplessly, as Arthur's mouth began to twist and shake. He mustn't have shaved for about three days . . .

'Aah'll away and tell Prudie. She'll be glad to know you're safe.' Realization dawned in his eyes. 'You might've been *killed*, Miss Anne! All you bairns might have been killed, and here Aah am fretting over a stupid old horse. Are ye all all right?'

'Yes,' said Timmo. 'But I'm afraid your shovel's under that lot.' He stared at the cliff-fall. 'There must be hundreds of tons of it.'

'Aye. Aah give the Watch House a year now. A year left, no more.' And Arthur was gone, struggling up the loose soil.

'The rotten bastard,' said Timmo. 'The rotten murderous stinking bastard.'

'Who – *Arthur*?' Anne looked at him in amazement.

'No,' said Timmo. '*You-know-who.*'

Anne glanced nervously up the cliff, as if it might start to fall again.

'Oh, the cunning swine,' said Timmo. 'Don't you *realize*! His bones are buried under this lot. We can't hope to dig them out again. The tide will take them and scatter them, and he'll be around for ever, now. He's *won*.'

'Yes,' said Anne. 'He's won. He got at the Gallower like he got at that dog . . .'

211

And then – and it was really frightening – a terrible knowing grin crossed Timmo's face. 'No, he hasn't. I've *got* him. I've *got* him. Oh, why didn't I think of it before?' The next second he was running like mad up towards Garmouth.

Anne looked at Pat. 'Will he be all right?'

'I've seen that look before, ducky. He'll be all right.'

22

'Aah don't know what we'll do for the fish,' said Prudie. 'Aah don't, Aah'm sure. Aah suppose Arthur could buy a bicycle, but it would give him a heart-attack, bicycling about at his age.' But she was pretty cheerful, really. She kept on making cups of tea. She had spent all her life preparing against a rainy day, and now it had come, she felt justified, in a mysterious way.

'Hey,' said Pat. 'Here's a police car. My God, and another.' There was a loud knocking on the cottage door.

'Are the two young ladies who saw the skeleton here?' asked the authoritative voice of the law.

A police-sergeant took them gingerly down the cliff. 'I want you to tell me exactly where the bones were when the cliff came down. They were in an old fish-sack, I gather?'

Above, a large yellow lorry had arrived, marked *Garmouth District Council.* Workmen, stripped to the waist and whistling cheerfully, were putting up a tripod and pulley.

'By, they've been quick,' said the sergeant. 'And they're getting a bulldozer along from the sea-wall site.'

They prowled around the rocks, and Anne had just made up her mind that the sack with the bones was directly under the Gallower, when there was a tremendous grinding and snorting. There was the bulldozer, on the Black Middens itself; heaving, straining, smashing the rock-edges to pulp, but getting to them slowly.

'Right,' said the sergeant. 'Well, we'll have you young ladies out of the way, now. You've been a great help, but we must hurry. We've only got three hours till the tide comes in; and if that bulldozer gets stranded, the Town Clerk'll be making buttons.'

They watched the bulldozer make its first, curiously-delicate cut at the tumbled soil, then retired to a decent distance. At the top of the cliff, they were joined by an exultant Timmo.

'*That'll* show the bastard.'

'What did you *do*?'

'I told Dad about the skeleton, and Dad rang the Coroner. The Coroner's a mate of Dad's. And he's responsible for all dead bodies discovered. He's duty-bound to recover them, investigate them, and hold an inquest on how they died. These gentlemen in blue you see before you, are not the policemen they seem. They have become, until the body is recovered, Coroner's Officers.'

It didn't take long. The poor body of the Gallower was born unceremoniously away on the blade of the bulldozer. Then the spade was recovered, then the bowl, and finally, the bag with the skeleton. There were several more minor cliff-falls, curiously near the work-site, but the bulldozer just ate them up.

'Our friend's still *trying*,' said Timmo, viciously. 'But I rather think he's bitten off more than he can chew.'

214

The sergeant came up with the bag. 'It all seems intact. I hope you're satisfied, young Jones? Giving us all this bother.'

'I'm satisfied if you are, sergeant. Only . . . there wasn't a skull. I searched the whole place, but there was no sign of a skull. Taking the bones for size, though, I think I know where the skull *is*. It was found years ago, on the same spot. I'm sure you ought to take it. Walk this way . . .'

The sergeant made Arthur open the glass case. Arthur protested, but only feebly. The sergeant gave him a look and said, 'All bodies unless claimed by relatives are considered the property of the Crown.' Then he picked up the skull as if it was no more than a can of paint, and shoved it in the bag. He turned to go.

'Just one more thing, sergeant,' said Timmo. The sergeant paused in the doorway.

'Don't forget to fasten your seat-belt, sergeant. And please drive carefully.'

'Less of your lip, young Jones,' said the sergeant, and left.

Timmo shook his head dolefully. 'He'll never realize how sincere I was. On the other hand, perhaps he just might.'

A week later, Anne and Pat were trying Mr Antonioni's patience. They had been in his shop two hours, had consumed two plain ices, and had twelve pence left between them.

'Let's ask for one with two spoons,' said Pat with a giggle. 'He's getting a big restive. We don't want to spoil his siesta.'

Anne giggled as well. It had been a week of giggles and nothing else. Except that Daddy had written to Prudie, thanking her for her kindness, and asking her to be kind a little longer, as he had to think. Daddy had also written to Anne, asking if she *really* wanted to live with *him*, and who would look after her if she did? The rest of the letter was about the Swedish rally-driver and Malcolm, who was still being hopeful in Stockholm.

'Men,' sighed Pat, 'are a nuisance. And here's the biggest nuisance of them all.'

Timmo bounced in, holding a copy of the *Garmouth Weekly News*, and looking like a cat with two tails.

'Look,' he said to Anne, and jammed the small-ads under her nose. One had a ring of red felt-tip round it.

Wanted. Good home for elderly Galloway pony. Still fit for light work. Cheap to right person. Apply Williamson, Preston North Farm.

'Who's Williamson?' asked Pat suspiciously.

'Friend of Dad's. And the pony's not *really* elderly. He's only seven. We had a hell of a job getting him. It's a well-baited trap for Arthur. Does he read the *Garmouth News*?'

'*Read* it?' said Anne. 'He *eats* it. Down to the printer's name, at the bottom of the back page.'

'Just make sure he doesn't miss this.'

'But he can't afford it. *Ponies* cost *money*.'

'Not this one. Fifteen quid to a good home.'

'Who's paying *really*?'

'Me, partly. After all, it was mainly my fault – my idea to dig up old Hague. I sold my moped.'

216

'Oh, *Timmo!*' Anne's eyes were shining so brightly that Timmo looked away.

'It's all right. I've got two more mopeds; and good old Dad put his hand in his pocket, too. But that's not the *best* news.' He turned the paper inside out, and pointed again.

CHAPTER OF ACCIDENTS LAID TO REST.

They're breathing a big sigh of relief at Garmouth Police Station tonight, because a parcel of old bones was buried in Garmouth Cemetery this morning. The bones were found by Garmouth schoolboy, Timothy Jones, on the Black Middens (see our previous edition), and since then, as Station-Sergeant Ken Smith says, 'It's been one damn thing after another.'

First the cliff collapsed, burying the bones, and they had to be dug out by a bulldozer loaned by Garmouth District Council. Then the police car taking them to the mortuary was involved in a slight collision.

Then they were transferred to a second police car, after a mongrel dog had tried to steal his dinner from the wreck. Then the second police car broke down.

Then they were transferred to a third police car, which also broke down. The bones were finally delivered to the mortuary on foot by PC Keith Harbridge, who lives at 9, Station Approach. Harbridge, in his turn, was followed by three mongrel dogs in search of a meal. 'They got quite insistent,' he said. 'I was glad I had my truncheon with me.'

Then the mortuary caught fire in the middle of the night; but Garmouth Fire Brigade dealt with the blaze before it could take hold.

Sergeant Smith commented, 'This guy, whoever he was, must have been a real Jonah. It's little wonder

217

the ship he was sailing sank. The captain must have regretted ever having him aboard.'

Cemetery Superintendent 'Cem' Jones commented, *'Well, he's six foot under now; we don't usually have any bother with residents.'*

The bones are thought to have belonged to a sailor drowned in one of the many shipwrecks on the Black Middens. The Coroner sitting on Tuesday, said the bones belonged to a man of about thirty-five years of age, and of gigantic stature. As far as could be judged, they were over a hundred years old, and matched a skull discovered at the same time by police, in Garmouth Volunteer Life Brigade Watch House. One curious feature of the autopsy was that the skeleton was found to be complete, apart from the bones of the right hand, which were entirely absent.

There were accompanying photographs of Station-Sergeant Ken Smith giving the thumbs-up sign, PC Keith Harbridge holding up his truncheon, and Cemetery Superintendent Cem Jones, looking firm.

'Well,' said Pat.

'He tried hard enough,' said Anne.

'But,' said Timmo, 'man or ghost, once you're caught up in the machinery of the English Law . . . the Law's like a bloody great steamroller. Not very fast, but impossible to stop. He'll need more than a dog to dig him out now; he'd need to jinx a bulldozer.'

'Oh, stop it,' said Pat. 'I once read a horrible short story where a ghost took over a bulldozer.'

'Science fiction, girl. Pure science fiction. Face it, the party's over. All cleared up once Anne gets Arthur to stick his head in the small-ads tonight.'

But, convinced that it was all over, they were overcome by a certain perversity.

'Let's go and have a last look at the Watch House,' said Pat.

They were really merry as they walked down the hill. Timmo started doing silly walks; Hitler goose-stepping; Charlie Chaplin; the Hunchback of Notre Dame. Pat kept exploding and saying, 'Oh, *stop* it! Everybody's staring!' in a way designed to make him worse. One passer-by laughed so much she nearly pushed her pram over in the gutter.

The Watch House dreamed peacefully in the never-ending sun. Arthur had cleared the remains of the figurehead off the lawn, and tipped them over the cliff. There hadn't been a piece left bigger than firewood.

The rocket-room baked comfortably. Pat ran her finger along a show case, and held it up showing a thin grey streak. 'Look how dusty it's got again. And to think of the hours we spent.'

But Anne didn't answer. Across the top of the next show case, someone had written in the dust, AN HELP PLEAS. It was fainter than before; but perhaps that was because the dust hadn't had time to gather.

'Oh, *fiddle*,' said Timmo, bored. 'Maybe it just got missed out in the dusting.'

'Maybe not,' said Anne. 'We might as well try again.' She began pushing the three armchairs into a circle. The old quiver was back in her stomach. She realized she'd rather missed it. Almost professionally, now, they settled down in the old routine.

*

Two hours later Anne got up and stretched. It was late, nearly tea-time. Shadows were starting to gather in the corners of the rocket-room. It was September now; nights were drawing in.

'Same thing again,' she said. 'He's just repeating himself. It's not even very clear, or exciting. Maybe he's losing interest too.'

'Tell us all the details again,' said Timmo, yawning.

'There's this little steamer aground on the Long Sands. The *Margaret A* of Hull. She's not in any real danger because it's all sand there, and she's facing bows-on to the waves anyway. The Brigade's trying to get the horse and cart with the rockets down onto the beach. They're trying to dig a ramp down a grassy bank from the sea front; just next to one of those little ornamental bandstands – you know, the sort the Victorians liked so much. The Old Feller's not worried about the ship. But he is worried about the digging. The men are digging right next to the bandstand, and the sand is coming out from under the bandstand's foundations. He keeps trying to move the men to one side. Perhaps he's scared the bandstand will topple over and the Town Council will want compensation . . .'

'Doesn't sound very likely,' said Timmo. 'Is there any danger of the bandstand toppling over?'

'No-ooo. It's quite wide really. They'd have to really dig underneath it before it tipped over . . .'

'Then that's not the reason. Maybe there's something . . . Oh, Jemima!'

'What?' The two girls looked at him, suddenly tense.

220

'Maybe there's something buried under the band-stand that the Old Feller doesn't want them to find.'

'Like what?'

'Like Hague's ditty-box and . . . Hey, where's that photograph?'

He went along the room like a whirlwind, looking at the pictures on the walls. He vanished up the stair-case, and there was a shout. They hurried after him.

He had paused on the first landing, in front of a picture-frame. It held six brown faded photographs of ships in various stages of distress.

'I *thought* what you said rang a bell. Here she is. *The* MARGARET A. *of Hull, ashore on the Long Sands, April 20th 1892*. The crew of eight were all saved by breeches-buoy, including the Captain's wife and two-year-old son. But the ship, in spite of efforts to refloat her, became a total write-off. Her keelplates and boiler are still visible on the sands at low tide. I know that boiler like the back of my hand. I remember larking about inside, when I was a kid. The band-stand's gone, but . . . hey, where does Arthur keep that shovel?'

'Roy Rogers rides again,' sneered Pat, 'on his favourite horse Trigger. Played by yours truly.' But the catchy excitement was in her voice too.

'*No*,' said Anne emphatically.

'What do you mean, no?'

'I don't like it. I've got a nasty feeling . . .'

'Oh, don't be such a spoilsport,' said Pat.

'I'll get my own shovel,' said Timmo. 'C'mon, Pat.'

Anne stood and listened while their excited voices faded, not knowing what to do. But the fear grew and grew in her mind. Why should it? The Old Feller's last message had been such a dull little message . . . The shadows darkened in the long room; but she was not afraid of the shadows. The danger was no longer in the Watch House.

She turned and ran. To the Roman Catholic Presbytery.

'By gum, the beach is empty,' said Timmo.

They were much later than they had hoped. Timmo's mother had asked them whether they'd had tea, and Timmo, in a foolish moment, had said they hadn't time for tea. Mrs Jones had insisted on feeding them. Dr Jones had insisted on telling Pat, who was rather a favourite of his, about the mysteries of propagating vegetable marrows. The marrows had been inspected in great detail. It was really dusk by the time they had managed to get rid of him, and pinch his best spade from the garden shed.

They had met the last sun-wearied holidaymakers climbing off the beach. Dads festooned like Christmas trees with rubber rings, buckets, spades and windbreaks. Mums checking beach-bags as they walked, for cameras and purses. Children whose legs glinted with encrusted sand. Now they walked through the wreckage of the day's battlefield. Jumped-on sandcastles, punctured beachballs; milk-bottles full of wet sand. But already the tide was sweeping in to clear it all up. Litter, fresh as today's newspaper; the sea as old as time.

'There's the boiler,' said Timmo. 'Hey, isn't the *light* funny?'

Pat looked. It kept darkening and brightening.

'It's the clouds,' said Timmo. 'We're in the shadow of the cliffs here, so it's dusk. But the sunlight's still on the clouds, and when a big cloud comes over, the light reflects down.'

'*Thank you*, Professor Einstein. Don't ring us; we'll ring you.'

But Timmo was looking at the sloping grassy bank between the beach and the sea-front. 'Aye-*aye*! Look, Pat. Under the putting-green.'

A putting-green had been built out level to the sand's edge. Its seaward side was held from crumbling by a four-foot wall of rustic stone. Its turf was bone-dry, and its little metal markers had been twisted by generations of putters. Timmo was pointing under the marker that said '9'.

'See, under the base of the wall.'

Pat looked. Jutting out from the base of the wall, buried in the base of the wall, was a lump of orna-mental cast-iron, red with rust. Four yards to the left was another.

'They must have pulled down the bandstand and built the putting-green over it. But if we dig we can still get *under* the bandstand. Let's try the right-hand side first.'

A few thrusts of the spade made a big cavern under the wall. The sand was bone-dry, and hissed off the spade as he shovelled.

'Look.'

The corner of a metal box was showing, rusty but intact.

'The dry sand under the bandstand must have preserved it,' said Timmo.

223

The box came out easily. It was small enough to be carried in the hand, but terribly heavy.

'I'll bust it open with the shovel. Stand back.'

'It's not locked,' said Pat. The lid moved under her hand, with a slight grating noise.

Timmo looked round, suddenly furtive. 'Hurry up and open it then,' he said. 'There's somebody coming. Look, down by the water's edge. Guy in a red jumper.'

Pat lifted the lid.

23

The door of the Presbytery opened, and Anne saw a
pair of sturdy female legs in thick grey stockings. Her
eyes panned up over a dark blue dress with tiny
sprigged flowers, and came to a square face, with
grey hair pulled back into a tight bun. The woman's
dark eyes, set close together, were assessing, experienced and hostile.

'What you want?' The accent was unashamedly
Irish.

'Can I see Father da Souza, please?'

'He's not in. He's out.'

'When will he be back?'

'That's none of my business, and it's none of yours.'

'Please, it's *terribly* important.'

'*Really*? Are you a Catholic?'

'No.'

The face, if possible, grew harder. 'The Father's
out, and I've no idea when he'll be back.'

She shut the door. Anne had the terrible idea that
she would have said Father da Souza was out, even
if he had been in. He might be inside now, reading
or just drinking tea. Or he might be walking with
Father Fletcher a hundred yards away, in the Priory
grounds. She wondered whether she should go and
search the Priory grounds. But then Father da Souza

might come home and enter this terrible impenetrable door while she was away searching.

So she just stood, paralysed. Three No. 11 buses went past to Newcastle. Four came past from Newcastle. They only ran every ten minutes. Time was slipping away from her. If only Father da Souza would come. But he was probably settled in the Presbytery for the night.

She turned and looked at the black façade of the house. Immediately a lace curtain twitched. She was being watched, and she knew who was watching. It gave her an idea. She set her mouth firmly, and sat down on the Presbytery steps.

It had the desired effect. The lace curtain twitched six times, at decreasing intervals, and then the door opened.

'Get off those steps. This is a respectable house. What do you think people will say, you sitting on those steps like that? Don't they teach you no shame in *your* church?'

Anne almost said she had no church; then realized it wouldn't have helped.

'I am sitting here waiting for Father da Souza.' Anne turned her back and sat down again.

The woman shuffled behind her, as if contemplating ejecting her by force. Then the door slammed again. But the curtain went on twitching. Passers-by stared at Anne, as if she was some kind of freak. But she went on sitting. She watched the minute-hand of her watch crawling round.

Then the door opened again. An elderly male voice said, 'Thank you, Mrs O'Malley, you may leave this to me, now.' She turned in confusion, and saw two long, thin legs in black trousers. Then a black clerical front, and a clerical collar. But it wasn't Father da Souza.

'I think you had better come this way.' The voice was cold and wary; a voice expecting hysterics and planning how to deal with them. The voice objected to her jeans and her T-shirt and practically everything about her. She walked up a dark, cold polished hall, and into a dark, cold polished study.

'Sit down, please. There. Now, what is the trouble? I cannot have you upsetting Mrs O'Malley like this.'

'I must see Father da Souza.' Anne still couldn't look at the man. She stared at the polished desk-top, with its copy of the Douai Bible and other strange, heartless foreign objects.

'How do you know Father da Souza? You are not a Catholic.'

'I met him in the Priory with Father Fletcher. I'm in Father Fletcher's youth club.'

'Then if you are one of Father Fletcher's flock, you had better go and see him.'

'Oh, he's nice. But he wouldn't *understand*. Father da Souza *understands*.'

'You would be surprised how many women, not all of them young, alas, share your conviction that Father da Souza is the only *man* who understands them. I suggest you contact Father Fletcher. You may use my telephone for the purpose, if you wish. You do seem distressed.'

At that first note of compassion, Anne looked at his face. It was a harsh face, and lined. Not lined like Prudie's face, though; or Arthur's, or even Bosun Mason's. Not a mass of wrinkles. Just a few deep black lines round the mouth and brow, that seemed to have been pencilled in over and over again. An iron face; as impenetrable as the front door of the Presbytery.

'Father Fletcher won't *do*. Oh, he knows about the Watch House a bit . . .'

'*Are you the child from the Watch House?*'

'Yes,' said Anne, wondering.

The next second, the old priest was running for the door. There was an urgency in his running that made Anne even more afraid.

'Money,' said Pat, aghast.

The tin box was full of small, fat gold coins.

'Sovereigns,' said Timmo. 'I've only seen a sovereign once. My grandfather had one on his watch-chain for a decoration, when I was little.' They both stood staring. 'Sovereigns are worth about twenty pounds each. There's a fortune here. Treasure trove, of course, unless they can prove who the owner is.'

'There's a bit of paper. See what it says.'

Timmo unfolded the brown slip. '*I have paid in full. Henry Cookson.*'

'What does he mean, paid in full?'

'I don't know.'

'See if there's anything else.'

Timmo plunged his hand in among the fat coins, scrabbled deep, and then pulled his hand out quickly, and pushed it under his armpit.

'What *was* it?'

'Nothing, Pat, nothing.' His voice sounded jumpy, strange.

'What *was* it?' On the edge of panic, she pushed

228

her own hand in. Timmo's hand fastened round her wrist like a vice, and pulled her fingers from out of the gold.

'What *was* it?' She was screeching now.

'Bones. Bones still fastened together. Let's get the box back under cover. We can come back in the morning. Where's that guy got to, down by the water's edge? He'll be nosing up here in a minute?'

She looked down the beach. The light faded again, as the cloud overhead passed out to sea. But she could still see an upright shape, a dark, upright shape, outlined against the foam of the waves, approaching.

Then a bigger wave than the others pushed inland in a swelling surge of foam. The kind that catches you and soaks your feet if you don't dodge quickly.

But the figure didn't dodge. Didn't react at all as the wave buried him to the knees. It was wrong, that; hard to believe. Not human, not to react at all.

'Timmo.' She grabbed at his arm, as the figure looked towards them. Left the water's edge, and began walking up to the putting-green.

Urgent muttering in the hall. The old priest's voice cautioning, almost querulous. Father da Souza's explosive with impatience.

'I *must* go with her. You know this is a bad case. You agreed it was serious.'

'It is either children's nonsense or very serious indeed. If it's nonsense, you will be making a fool of yourself. You know how people gossip about us. These children are not even Catholic.'

'And if it is serious?'

'Then only exorcism will serve. And that is a matter for the Bishop.'

'Who will spend three months humming and hawing. It's happening *now*, Father.'

'Then ring your friend Fletcher.'

'Fletcher . . .' There was a universe of gentle condemnation in that word. And gentle desperation, because Father da Souza sounded quite frantic; like a bird beating its wings against the bars of its cage. 'I must go *now*.'

'I forbid you. I am in charge of you. You will obey me in *all things*.'

'I will disobey you in this thing. And do penance for it afterwards.'

'That is a sin against the Holy Spirit.'

'Then the Holy Spirit will have to forgive me, too.'

'Oh, you young priests . . .'

Father da Souza burst into the study, his face sweating and livid with an emotion Anne couldn't fathom. 'Serious?' he asked.

'Serious,' said Anne. 'Timmo and Pat have gone. I couldn't stop them.'

'Where?'

'The Long Sands.'

'Come on. You can tell me all about it as we go.' He had a black book in his left hand. He grabbed her wrist with his right; hard. They bundled out into the hall. The old priest was leaning back against the hall table, grasping its edge with both hands. He looked pale and ill.

'Pray,' shouted Father da Souza at him, and it sounded like an order. Then he pulled Anne towards the front door.

230

The old priest's voice followed them.

'An exorcism needs *two* priests . . .'

But they were gone. Passers-by stopped, stared and turned on their heel to watch the remarkable sight of a Catholic priest in a cassock running hand-in-hand with a dishevelled teenage girl.

I must have more charity, thought the old priest. I must make greater efforts to understand the young. He went back to his cold, polished study and knelt down. But the moment he knelt, he knew he ought to be up and *doing* something. Yet when he got up, he knew he ought to kneel and pray. After he had knelt and got up for the third time he made up his mind. He muttered something that an unbeliever might have heard as '*Damn* the Bishop.' He went to a small, dirty leather case that stood in one corner of the room and checked its contents. Then, holding it firmly, he turned towards the door.

Before you come to the Long Sands at Garmouth, you come to the Short Sands, which is a little curving bay lined by deep cliffs. The sea-front promenade runs round the top. As the old priest reached the near end, he saw the tiny figures of Anne and Father da Souza vanish round the far end. They seemed very far away; an infinity away. Panic seized the old priest. He would never catch them. Everything was slipping out of his grasp. He began to run, and he hadn't run for years.

He was vaguely surprised his legs could still move like that. But they seemed far away; a collection of joints no longer part of him, and getting further away all the time. His rasping breath caught in his throat.

231

He began coughing uncontrollably. He veered sideways and bumped into the promenade railings. He clung to them for support, feeling the layers of rust under the fresh white paint.

'Father! Are you all right?' An honest, round female face, full of concern, swam into his vision. One of his parishioners, Mrs . . . Mrs . . . he couldn't remember.

'Come and sit down, Father.' She led him to one of the cliff-top seats. A crowd gathered. 'The Father's had a nasty turn.'

One of the men said he had his car handy; he would run the Father home in a jiffy . . .

'Car, please . . .' the old priest managed to get out, before that awful coughing started again. He wanted to use the car to follow da Souza.

But they bundled him into it, and drove him home. And Mrs O'Malley bustled out, and said how she'd warned the Father he was Doing Too Much, but he would never listen. He never Spared Himself and was up doing good at All Hours. And now it had Come to This.

The old priest tried to raise his hand and tell them. But his voice was low and hoarse with the coughing. And everyone else was so sure they knew what was best, and said so in the loudest voices.

The dirty, little leather case lay where it had fallen, back by the railings. Nobody noticed it, until a boy brought it back to the Presbytery next day.

'Go on, run,' said Timmo. 'Go and fetch help. I'll cope with this.' His voice sounded very odd.

But Pat stayed kneeling where she was. 'I can't. My legs won't work.'

'Turn your back, then. Close your eyes. Don't look.'

She shuffled herself round awkwardly, to face the low wall of the putting-green. But she couldn't bear to close her eyes. She stared at the half-dead dandelions that fringed its top. And the little metal marker saying '9'. Up there was freedom, Mum, home, No. 11 buses, roaring coal fires. Safety. But the four-foot wall might as well have been the walls of Troy.

Next second, two figures were flying straight at her; one black, one blue. She nearly screamed, until she realized it was Anne and Father da Souza. *Thump, thump*, they went, into the soft sand behind her.

Father da Souza's voice came calm and clear. 'Don't *look*, Timmo. Don't look, Anne. Look down at the sand. He *wants* you to look at him. He lives on fear.'

There was a silence, a near unbearable silence that almost compelled you to look. Pat could feel Timmo's legs, pressed against her own back; the legs were trembling.

Then Father da Souza said, 'I don't suppose anybody's got a cross?'

Pat fumbled inside her sweater for the cheap tawdry thing she had taken to wearing. She had won it at a shooting-stall on a fairground. The weak chain snapped, because her hand was so tense. The cross fell in the sand, and there was an awful moment when she thought she'd lost it. Then she held it out blindly, and said, 'Will this do?'

'It will do very well. Is anybody here a Christian?'

'Don't look at me,' said Timmo, with a flicker of his old spirit.

233

'I don't *know*,' said Anne helplessly.

'I am,' said Pat.

'I need your help,' said Father da Souza. 'There should always be two for this kind of thing.'

'But I'm Chapel . . .' said Pat.

'That doesn't matter. Come round beside me. *No* – don't *look up*. Just try to pray – anything. But don't try making prayers up in your head. Say prayers you've been taught – ones you know by heart. Be careful you get the words right. Say them over and over again.'

'*Lord bless this food to our use and us to Thy service*,' mumbled Pat. Ridiculous. Then one from the depths of childhood: '*Gentle Jesus meek and mild.*' Ridiculous again. Kid's stuff. And all the time that awful thing must be listening to her . . . unless it had gone and she was babbling to empty air . . . she tried a quick peep.

'Look *down*,' roared Father da Souza.

She pulled her eyes back from that ambush just in time. And settled at last into a monotonous rhythm of the Lord's Prayer.

'Good,' said Father da Souza. 'Now the rest of you, leave this to me. I can look at him. I've been trained for it. Say your twelve-times table, if you can find nothing better.'

When he spoke again, his voice was cold and technical.

'In the name of the Father, Son and Holy Ghost, I adjure you to tell me your name.'

Silence.

'You may signify assent by nodding your head. Your name is Scobie Hague.'

It wasn't a question, but a statement.

'Major Scobie Hague, late of the Fifty-fifth Regiment of Foot.'

Silence.

'Cashiered from your regiment in Australia for cheating at cards.'

Pat gasped. How could Father da Souza have learnt that?

'Who fled from Australia because the Governor of New South Wales had issued a warrant for your arrest, in connection with the murder of a convict named Joseph Shears and his wife.'

Pat gasped again. So much for Major Hague the selfless hero foully done to death.

'Who fled from the sinking *Hoplite* with gold you had stolen, property of the Union Bank, London.'

Pat thought hazily that Father da Souza's voice was like an axe. A sharp axe cutting down a tree. With every stroke a branch fell: a branch made of pride, or arrogance, of righteous grievance. With every stroke, the ghost of Scobie Hague must be getting smaller. But still the awful silence continued.

'Who murdered Joseph Beavers and George Dobie on the Black Middens, on the night of the 14th of October 1854.'

Silence.

'Hero?' asked Father da Souza. 'Hero? You were saving no one but yourself. *Your* gold? Gold you had stolen.'

Silence.

'Furthermore, you plagued the body and soul of Henry Cookson, in life and in death. What right have you to judge the living and the dead? Vengeance is

235

mine; I will repay, saith the Lord. It is your own sins you must think of now, Scobie Hague. It is your own sins you will shortly have to answer for.'

Silence. A silence like steel grating on steel.

'Do you repent? It will be easier for you if you repent. You may signify by a nod.'

Silence.

'Very well.' There was the slightest trace of regret in Father da Souza's voice. 'Timmo, can you dig a hole in the sand?'

Timmo was fighting his own growing temptation to look. It was babyish not to look. To be *told* not to look, like a child at a street accident. Father da Souza was *looking*, wasn't he? What was so superior about Father da Souza? Timmo's eyes crept across the sand, footprint by footprint. Only a little peep at the creature's feet . . .

'Timmo! Don't look. *Dig*!'

Timmo began resentfully scooping out the sand with one hand.

'Please hurry,' said Father da Souza. Suddenly he sounded like a man holding up one corner of a grand piano, waiting for someone else to slip a carpet underneath it. Timmo began using two hands together, as he had as a little boy on the same beach long ago. Soon he was a foot down, among the damp stuff.

'That will do,' said Father da Souza. 'Now, is there a hand in that box? Ah, I thought as much, after that coroner's inquest report. Can you get it out and put it in the hole?'

The silence grew and swelled inside Timmo's head, like the silence before a thunderstorm. He put his own hand on top of the gold coins and began to push the coins about feebly; not wanting to reach far enough down. He had a sudden terrible fear that if he touched the bundle of skin-bound bones down there, it would fasten round his own hand like a crab and never let go.

'Hurry,' said Father da Souza, with a little gasp. But Timmo couldn't move.

Then he heard Pat start mumbling the Lord's Prayer again.

'*Lead us not into temptation, but deliver us from evil.*'

Timmo grabbed the dead hand and a mass of coins together and threw them down the hole.

'Do you *still* refuse to repent?' asked Father da Souza.

Silence.

'Fill up the hole, Timmo.'

Timmo began pushing in the sand. He expected the hand to go frantic, like a crab, and start scrabbling up the sides of the hole in an attempt to escape. But it stayed still, and slowly vanished.

'Good,' said Father da Souza, and then the Latin started. It was like great chains, strong ropes.

The whole beach seemed to lift and throw itself at them. Pebbles beat into Timmo's face like hailstones. He pulled up the hood of his anorak and crouched into a tight ball with his hands over his head. But he could hear the Latin going on and on.

The pebbles stopped. Timmo was just about to look up when there was a hiss and a swish. Something large hit Father da Souza with a thump. The priest grunted in pain, and a piece of rotting driftwood fell on the sand. Another swish and another. Every missile was finding its mark. Once Father da Souza dropped his black book. When he reached down to recover it there was blood on his hand. It was awful having to crouch there and listen to the priest being beaten up.

But then the Latin seemed to reach an important place. The priest's voice said something three times, and each time his voice got more triumphant.

Then the sandstorm came. Hissing, cutting, reaching through clenched fingers, through closed eyelids.

The Latin stopped.

'I . . . can't . . . see,' said Father da Souza.

Silence. Then Pat said shakily, 'What's happening?'

'Keep still,' said Father da Souza. 'Don't move, whatever you do. It will pass.'

Then they heard the footsteps approaching, squeaking across the sand. From behind. Timmo bit into a fat fold of his anorak, just to stop himself screaming and flying into a thousand pieces. Grains of sand from the anorak grated between his teeth. They tasted of salt. He could see Anne's hands clenched against each other; like hands of stone.

'I . . . I . . . had a phone call from the Presbytery,' said Father Fletcher. 'What can I do?'

'The book,' said Father da Souza. 'Halfway down the right-hand column of the left-hand page. Read from there.'

Father Fletcher read. His Latin didn't flow like Father da Souza's. He pronounced a lot of words oddly. You could tell he hadn't read Latin for a very long time. But Father da Souza kept on chipping in with a bit to help him, and he made it, right down to the last *In nomine Patris, et Filii et Spiritus Sancti, Amen.*'

238

'All right,' said Father da Souza. 'It's over. You can all get up now.'

Timmo came to with a start. He had fallen into a kind of glazed exhaustion. He looked around. It was nearly dark, but there was enough light to see the beach was completely empty. Father da Souza was putting something away in a pocket in the skirts of his cassock.

But Anne was staring fixedly at something Timmo couldn't see.

'Oh, *no*!' he groaned in despair. 'After all that . . .'

'Don't worry,' said Father da Souza, still wiping sand from his eyes. 'She's smiling. There's no more need for us here. Come on. I'll buy you a Coke.'

'You couldn't run to a beer?' asked Timmo.

'My good friend, Father Fletcher does not sell spiritous liquors.'

They stiffly climbed the low wall, onto the dry turf of the putting-green. Leaving Anne behind worried Timmo a bit. But Father da Souza must know best. He was the professional.

Timmo was silent all of fifty yards. Then he said, 'How d'you know all that about Hague? That Australian stuff?'

'The Public Records Office is a wonderful place. Especially when you have a Jesuit friend living in London with too much time on his hands. I have photostats of all Hague's army records. I even knew how much he drew as ration-allowance on the third of March 1850. Of course, that newspaper account of the wreck of the *Hoplite* started me off.'

'So you *were* spying on Anne that day in the Priory?'

239

'Call it pastoral care.'

'With binoculars?'

'Why shouldn't the Church use the miracles of modern science?'

'The Church Technological. Us poor heathens can't win.'

They walked another fifty yards in silence.

'Anyway, you fixed Hague good and proper.'

'I fixed *something*.'

'What do you mean?'

'Perhaps it was the real Major Hague, cheated of his gold and his marriage. Trapped here on earth by his own rage for revenge. Or perhaps . . .' Father da Souza paused, as if wondering whether to continue, then said, 'perhaps the Old Feller *made* Hague. Perhaps Hague was part of the Old Feller all the time.'

'You mean he made him up? Funny that. Hague *was* a bit like a ten-year-old's bogey-man . . . all that stuff about eyes dropping out of skulls . . . childish really.'

'No, I don't mean he made him up; I mean he *made* him. Out of the guilt, festering in his lonely mind all those years.'

'You mean the Old Feller never told anyone about the murder he saw?'

'Well, there's no record of anyone being tried for Hague's murder. As his memorial said, everyone went on regarding Hague as a hero drowned at sea.'

'So what d'you think happened?'

'I think the Old Feller stayed hidden in his crevice in the rocks while the wreckers cut Hague's hand off and slipped his body back in the sea. Then he

240

followed the wreckers when they carried off the ditty-box, shared out the loot, and buried the ditty-box under the bandstand. Then the Old Feller went home perhaps, and managed to slip into bed without his parents missing him. He'd have been in terrible trouble if they'd found out what he'd done. Then he waited and . . . perhaps he *meant* to tell about what he'd seen. But the body was never found, and every day that passed it seemed more like just a bad dream. Without a body, who would have believed a child of ten anyway?'

'And then . . . ?'

'The ditty-box would play on his mind. Sooner or later he went back and dug it up. The hand was inside, and perhaps the wreckers had left two or three gold coins. Any child would have taken them . . . but once he had taken them, he felt as guilty as the wreckers. Then the nightmares would start. And he tried all his life to pay off his terrible debt. Replacing all those gold coins in the ditty-box out of his own pocket . . . no wonder he went bankrupt. And that poor little note: *I have repaid in full*. But he hadn't. Hague wouldn't go away. Then the Old Feller started the Life Brigade; built the piers . . . but nothing would ever finally satisfy the thing called Hague. I cannot begin to think what that man must have gone through . . .'

'And all for a childish bogey-man.'

'Do you know what bogey-men really are?'

''Course not. Psychological, I suppose.'

'Ever heard of the Devil?'

'Oh, go *on*!' Timmo was on the verge of sneering.

'I don't know what it was,' said Father da Souza.

'And I don't think I really want to know. I only know the whole thing was evil and getting bigger all the time. It was getting fed and getting stronger. At first it could only make footsteps, or knock things over. Then it could throw tumblers; then a whole ship's figurehead.'

'What was feeding it?'

'You people were. While it only had old men for company . . . old men who treated it as a joke . . . it was harmless. Then Anne came and she was lonely, missing her father. Wanting something to love and protect . . .'

'You mean it lured her in and *used* her?'

'Or she was using it . . . you can never tell with disturbed adolescent girls; a number have been the centres of poltergeist activity. When two people fall in love, who is using who?'

'That's *sick*!' burst in Pat angrily.

'Yes, it *is* sick, my dear,' said Father da Souza sharply. 'As your undue interest in tumbler-writing was sick and helped to feed the . . . creature. And Timmo's rage and cleverness and determination to beat the creature to a pulp. It was feeding on all of you.'

Timmo stopped abruptly, and looked back the way they had come. 'But you've left Anne there with it.'

'It will be all right. I covered all the permutations down there on the beach, just like in a football pool. Either I broke Hague's self-righteous rage; or the Old Feller's irrational fear; or the Devil, by the power of the Church. Only none of it was me,' he added hastily. 'It was all the power of the Church.'

'But can't we ever know?' asked Pat.

'Not really. Think of it as the Old Feller asking for help; asking for help against himself, like we all need.'

A car drew up behind them. A Rolls-Royce. Not a new Rolls-Royce; an 'H' registration. And certainly the dirtiest Rolls-Royce Timmo had ever seen. The grey bodywork, under the street-lights, was covered with black oily fingerprints from end to end.

A small grubby man got out, who matched the car. It was impossible to imagine he owned it; he must be delivering it.

'Excuse me,' said the man humbly. 'I wonder if you could tell me the way to the Watch House. My daughter is staying there.'

Pat opened her mouth. Father da Souza gave her the most discreet kick possible on the ankle.

'That is the Watch House down there, across the bay,' said Father da Souza. 'And those lighted windows behind are Brigade Cottage.'

'Thanks', said the man. He noticed Timmo looking at the Rolls. 'Quite nice, isn't she? Just bought her. Had to sell my last one, but I don't like being without a Rolls for long – they're a lovely bit of machinery. So when my luck turned, the first thing I did . . .' He shook his head, baffled. 'It's a funny business, the motorcar trade. One day nobody wants you, the next everyone's beating a path to your door. Good night!'

He got back into the Rolls and drove away down the bank.

'So now it *is* all over,' said Timmo.

'Yes, it's all over now,' said Father da Souza, nodding to where the lights of the Rolls were lighting up the white sides of the Watch House. 'It's over because that man has come. Anne will have a full-time job looking after *him* now. He's a good little man – just a bit baffled. It's a sad fact but true – it's always the unloved children who get into trouble. Like child-murders . . . you never get a *loved* child getting into a car with a strange man, no matter how many sweets he offers.'

'What about all that lovely lolly,' asked Timmo abruptly. 'The gold, I mean?'

Father da Souza clapped his hand to his head. 'The gold! We just left it lying there. What an incredibly unworldly lot we must be.'

'Perhaps the See of Canterbury,' said Father Fletcher, 'is more worldly than the See of Rome.' He held up the rusty ditty-box with a grim smile. 'I suppose it will be a treasure-trove?'

'No,' said Father da Souza. 'That note inside proves it belonged to the Old Feller. It will be part of his estate. And I happen to know his will left everything to . . . guess who?'

'Don't tell me,' said Timmo. 'The Life Brigade. Arthur will get his sea-wall after all.'

'Just like a fairy-story,' said Father da Souza sarcastically. 'Virtue rewarded. Vice punished. Happy ending.'

'You even had the Old Feller's will?' asked Timmo.

'My Jesuit friend went to Somerset House, too,' said Father da Souza.

'My God, you are a real pro!' said Timmo, admiring at last.

'I hope you mean what I *think* you mean,' said Father da Souza, punching him gently in the stomach. 'I'll just let my father-in-God know we're all in one piece, and then we'll go and have that Coke.'

The Old Feller showed faintly, like a photographic print coming up slowly in a dark room. Black on dark. The newly-lit light of the North Pier again blinked brightly through his face.

'It's all right now,' said Anne soothingly. 'Hague's gone.'

The Old Feller smiled tentatively; the smile had a hard job breaking through the worry-lines on his face.

'You're *free*,' said Anne. 'What will you do now? Go back to the Watch House or . . . ?'

The Old Feller looked frightened again.

'It wasn't your fault,' said Anne. 'You were only *ten*. What could you have done? And you've *paid*. Oh, you've paid a hundred times over. They'll understand up . . .'

The Old Feller made a questioning gesture outwards; a slight gesture that somehow encompassed the whole universe. Then he looked more frightened than ever.

Then he set his mouth; squared his shoulders as he must have done so often in life.

'It won't be any worse than rescuing the Russkies,' said Anne. 'They *will* understand.'

And then she was standing alone on the beach.

Author's Note

I always wanted to write a ghost story. But I dislike aimlessly malevolent spooks, who perform random series of tricks like glowing footprints, sudden chills and horrid shrieks, rather as bad comedians string together unrelated jokes.

A satisfactory spook should have a metabolism, a purpose and a modus operandi. Through the discovery of these, he should be outwittable. Human beings are spooks plus. Why shouldn't *they* sometimes win?

I felt the only way forward for me was to find an historic building with intriguing contents, and make my ghost manifest through these. My search ended on the cliffs at Tynemouth, where the Watch House stands, exactly as I've described it. It was in real danger from cliff-erosion when I was a boy, but has now been made safe by the local council. It is open to the public; enquire at Brigade Cottage!

But Garmouth isn't Tynemouth. All my characters are pure fiction. Tynemouth Volunteer Life Brigade is a highly efficient rescue team. When the survey vessel *Oregis* went aground in 1974, Brigade members were actually on the move before the *Oregis* struck on Battery Rocks. My thanks are due to the Brigade for the temporary fictional loan of their HQ, and in particular to the assistant secretary, Mr A. E.

Gardiner. Although he had no idea I was writing this book, it was his enthusiastic string of yarns that set me off. Some are included in this book.

The description of the wreck of the *Hoplite* leans heavily on *Chester Chronicle*'s account of a famous Victorian shipwreck: that of the steamship *Royal Charter* on the cliffs of Anglesey. My thanks are due to Mr Herbert Hughes, editor-in-chief, for giving me access to his archives, and to Miss Mary Brocklehurst, his secretary, for guiding me through them so smoothly.

Anyone interested in the misdeeds of wreckers will find a large Cornish literature on the topic. Murders, alas, did take place, mainly because of an old statute of the Plantagenet kings that a wreck was not lawful prey for looters while any of the crew and passengers remained alive.

R.A.W.

247

Stormsearch

I began to wave my arms at Uncle Geoff as he ran along the beach. My heart was in my mouth. I just knew that no matter if I lived to be a hundred, I would never find anything half so wonderful again.

When Tim finds an old model ship washed up on the beach after a magnificent summer storm he knows he's stumbled upon something special. The tiny vessel has a hidden cargo – a mysterious secret from the past that Tim must try to solve. The boat's lonely journey has lasted over a hundred years – and only Tim can finish its perilous story of shipwrecks, buried treasure and tragedy.

Robert Westall titles
available from Macmillan